WHERE THERE'S A WILL

CAROLYN FAULKNER

Published by Blushing Books
An Imprint of
ABCD Graphics and Design, Inc.
A Virginia Corporation
977 Seminole Trail #233
Charlottesville, VA 22901

Where There's a Will
Carolyn Faulkner

eBook ISBN: 978-1-63954-520-9
Print ISBN: 978-1-63954-521-6

1

"I want her out of here. Now. This minute."

Although he hadn't raised his voice, there was no mistaking just how passionate he felt about the issue, standing there in a suit that probably cost more than his first house, Thornton mused unkindly.

But then he sighed. "I don't know what you have against her. She's been a savior to me."

"Ha! A savior—that's rich! She's barely out of the gutter. She's not a nurse, even. She's just a nursing "assistant."

He held up his hand to interrupt. "I'm talking, and I'll thank you to shut up and listen while I do so. We don't speak much, but I'm going to talk a lot right now." He adjusted himself in his chair, his hips feeling uncomfortable but not wanting his son to realize that. "You know, I wasn't born yesterday and I haven't lost my marbles, despite what I know you consider to be my highly advanced age, and how much you'd truly enjoy that turn of events so that you could step into my shoes."

His son managed to look affronted at that comment, but Thornton didn't buy it.

"Before I hired her—almost a year ago, I'll remind you—I called all of her references and met her supervisor, who was in close contact with the both of us until I decided to hire her away from that agency and give her a better paid, full time position living here, with me." He gave his son a jaundiced look.

"Yes, I know where she used to live, and this certainly is a step up," the younger man sneered.

"You won't believe it, but I had to spend about four months trying to convince her to move in." His son outright snorted at that. "And don't you think I've had her investigated, as well as tested her honesty? I've left gold pens out on my desk that are worth more than she makes in a month. She's never touched them. As a matter of fact, one was under the desk and I didn't know it, and she gave it back to me. I've had girls in here taking care of me who would have gone out to lunch the first time I did that and never come back, with the pens in their pockets. I gave her my credit card number—"

Hugh looked alarmed at both things that had come out of his father's mouth. Apparently, he wasn't paying nearly enough attention to what was going on with his only remaining parent.

"—one with a very small limit, of course—to go buy a few things for me, and she handed me back the card, with the receipt, and I never saw anything else come through on the card that I hadn't asked her to buy. Hell, she flat out refused to become an authorized user on the account! My wallet is on my bedside every night—and you know I hate plastic money, so it always has about five hundred dollars in it. She's never touched it.

"She's trying to better herself, too. Besides being at my beck and call all hours of the day—even before she moved in—she's going to school to become a nurse." Smart, but world weary, rheumy eyes settled on his clear, piercing ones. "I'm well aware that she comes from the wrong side of the tracks. I'm also well aware that you have a tendency to forget that that's where I came from, too."

The foreboding frown deepened under his father's eye.

"I had nothing, growing up. We ate what your grandfather could shoot—deer, if we were very lucky, possum, even squirrel, if we weren't. And he hunted on the very land you're standing on." He could tell that his son was trying to suppress the urge to roll his eyes as he was subjected to a story he'd heard over and over again. "I was six feet at my tallest—although I've lost a few inches at my age—but if I'd had better nutrition when I was younger, I wouldn't have gotten rickets that bowed my legs and made me two inches shorter than I should have been."

He paused a minute to catch his breath. "I got what I have, young man—what *we* have—because I worked and scraped and saved and fought for it." The white head bowed as if he no longer possessed the strength to hold it up. "I missed your childhood because I was busy trying to make sure you had a better life. That's something I've regretted all my life—that I wasn't there for your first steps, didn't go to your plays or football games, that I wasn't anywhere near as involved in your growing up as I should have been. But now, you're making me see that I have even more to feel guilty and regretful about than just that. Perhaps if I hadn't become rich, if you hadn't been given everything you wanted all your life, without having to work for it, then maybe you would've turned out to be a better person. Someone with a bit of empathy, who's less suspicious of those whose lives have been much, much harder than yours."

He was glad to see that chiseled jaw flex in anger at his words.

Hugh wasn't a bad person; he could just be stubborn about things that didn't happen the way he wanted them to —or people who refused to do the same. He had more of an ego than he was entitled to, as far as his father was concerned. Not that he hadn't done good things with the company—he had. But he hadn't built it from scratch; he hadn't had to sacrifice for what he had—he'd come into it when it was already one of the largest privately owned companies in the country and made it even bigger, and, the old man admitted, better, more efficiently run.

Thornton Calumet rose, leaning on his cane much more than he wanted to in front of his big, powerful son, who reminded him so much of himself in so many ways—most of them physical. He was the absolute image of himself at that age—although Hugh was a big taller and more muscular than he had been.

He hadn't had the benefit of a gym right off his office, though.

But Thornton had done his best—as he'd become richer and more powerful—to reach back and raise up those who were behind him, those who needed a bit of help—money, a job, or even just a reference to a well-placed friend of his— to make better lives for themselves.

Hugh didn't have that quality, or, if he did, he'd hidden it damned well for somewhere around thirty years.

Not for the first time since he'd become sick, he wished he knew his son better than he did, although he was pretty much resigned to the fact that it was too late to rectify that situation.

"I'm afraid, son, that, since I have stubbornly—and, I'm sure you think, inconveniently—managed to hang around, the bottom line is that I still own everything, including the house you're standing in. The salary that you receive as the CEO of my company paid for the clothes you wear, the cars you drive, and makes you just that more attractive to the women you fuck, whom I'd wager probably have no idea that you don't really own anything yourself."

Thornton's eyes narrowed. "How that must gall you—a man who so obviously thinks quite a lot of himself."

Hugh grunted at that but remained standing there, big hands balled in his pockets, unnaturally still, looking down at the suddenly stark vision of his frail father, the man who had always starred as a larger than life figure in his mind.

Tentative, slow steps brought him 'round and got him—barely—to the door to his own study, where he turned to look back at his only progeny.

"She will stay until I say she should leave, Hugh. She's just about the only ray of sunshine in my life, and I won't give her up just because you don't like her."

"It's not that I don't like her, Father; it's just that I think she's likely to take advantage of you in your..." He searched his brain for a delicate way to say it, but there really wasn't one. "...weakened state."

"I'm old; that I'll give you. But I'm sharp as ever up here." He tapped his temple with an arthritic forefinger. "You don't think—at my age—that I can spot an opportunist? I was routing them out of my company—and my bed, even after your mother took me on—long before you were born, sonny boy."

That was a visual without which Hugh could have lived quite happily.

And damn, he hated it when his father used that nickname, in particular. Somehow, it made him feel like some young upstart, when he was pushing forty, for Chrissakes!

"And she is not one of them."

Hugh sighed. "Well, I guess, eventually, one or the other of us will be proven right."

Turning back to pass through the door, Thornton continued. "And I intend to be around to watch you eat that crow."

Despite how annoyed he was by the old man, Hugh rushed to stand in the doorway and offered, "Why don't I call Lisa to come help you, Father?"

Without stopping his excruciatingly slow progress, the other man threw back, "In lieu of you actually stooping to help me yourself? Yes, that would be preferable. At least I know she truly wants to help me, because she cares about me. All you want to do is help me into an early grave so you can have all of this for yourself."

Grinding his teeth together fit to break them, Hugh managed to remain silent as he watched his father totter gingerly across the large foyer. He'd already texted Lisa, who dutifully met him before he made it to the small elevator.

"There you are," he exclaimed as she looped her arm through his free one. Hugh's eyes narrowed as he noticed that she seemed to go to great lengths to make it look—and make his father feel—as if he was the one escorting her, not the other way around. "I knew you'd find me, even if my son couldn't be bothered to call for you."

"He did call me—he texted me."

He had to give her credit for telling his father the truth when he doubted she knew that he was watching and listening.

"What did you expect him to do—stand in the middle of the foyer and bellow for me? You wouldn't be at all happy with that, either."

His father stopped short, giving Lisa a look that Hugh

himself well recognized. "Don't get sassy with me, young lady."

"No, sir," she replied, tongue firmly in cheek, giving him a fond look.

"No, I expected that he'd help me himself, but I guess that's too much to ask of such a grand man such as himself."

There was a loud, unladylike snort, and just as the elevator doors closed, he heard, "As if you'd let him help you, even if he'd tried! You just wanted him to offer, so you could have the pleasure of turning him down!"

He had to admit he was somewhat touched—and very surprised—to hear her defending him to his father as well as calling the old man out quite astutely—and sharply—for his own skewed behavior.

Hugh shook his head. Those two actions hardly negated what he was quite certain was her goal—to get ahold of as much of the family money as she could. She was hardly the first woman to try to get at a family's fortune this way, but he intended to do everything he could—everything he felt he needed to—to stop that from happening, regardless of his father's reassurances.

LISA GUIDED Thornton to his room. He was already in his dressing gown and pajamas, having dressed himself, however slowly, in her presence earlier, before his much anticipated—and dreaded—meeting with his stubborn son.

And he wasn't the only one who wasn't too keen on his having a chat with that overblown jackass. Lisa had been quietly sitting in her room, which was next to Thornton's for convenience, wondering if she should be getting her things together to leave, while they were deciding her fate in the big study downstairs.

As she helped him lift his legs up onto the bed—really lifting very little in order to encourage him to continue strengthening his muscles, but rather just providing a bit of support for something he could do on his own—she asked, only half kidding, "So, am I expected to get outta here in the morning?"

She was unprepared for the old man's response. He reached up and grabbed her wrist—in a move she would have shaken off and gotten angry about if it was anyone but him—with a strength that was a throwback to how strong he must have been in his prime, probably as strong as his son looked. "Don't you even think about that!"

Lisa tugged sharply, and he let her go with not a little reluctance.

"Think about it?" she huffed, arranging his multitude of pillows behind him as he lay back against them. "I was planning on it! My bags are practically packed!"

He looked stricken. "No! I won't have it! What I say still goes in this house, whether or not Junior likes that idea!"

"He's not a junior," she commented blandly, hoping to calm him as she pulled the sheet up over him, which was all he liked at first when he went to sleep. Lisa also made sure that he had the rest of his covers easily at hand, along with the remotes for his TV and fan. She'd long since Velcroed the backs of them together so they would stop getting lost.

"Close enough," came his agitated grumble.

"Have you done your meds?"

Thornton glared up at her as she reached for the cup she'd already filled—the one with a flat base and a handle that he had less trouble holding on to, as well as a cover, so that he now rarely spilled anything on himself. "You know I haven't; I just got up here! And stop trying to change the subject." His tone was sharp, but she knew he wasn't really angry with her.

"I'm not trying to do that. I'm trying to get you into bed and to face reality. That man does not want me here, and I have to admit that I can see his point. I'm not really supposed to be here."

"You're damned well supposed to be here if I say you're supposed to be here." Then he blushed charmingly. "Sorry for the language."

That made her chuckle softly, and Thornton allowed himself to relax a bit at that. "Gee, I wonder where he gets his stubbornness from? Seems to me, the stink bomb doesn't fall far from the originating bullshit-filled mushroom."

"Do you think you could torture that metaphor a bit more for me?"

"You know I could!" She grinned.

That, too, was one of the reasons he liked this woman. She was smart—she didn't have an advanced degree, but she was well-spoken, and they had each taught each other a few new words every once in a while. Most of the ones he'd learned from her had to do with the world of computers and the internet—both of which he was less familiar with than he would like to be—but learning was learning.

Just as she was reaching to turn off the lamp on the nightstand, he caught her arm again, more gently this time.

"I won't let him drive you away, Lisa."

Her smile was much less confident than he wanted to see. "Well, I'm not going to allow myself to be that easily driven out, but blood is thicker than water, and time will tell."

Thornton didn't like hearing that from her any more than he did from his son.

"Not in his case, it isn't. And old age and cunning will always triumph over youth and skill."

She laughed at that, and he felt young again for a short moment. "In your case, I don't doubt it one bit. You've had decades more experience at being a stubborn old coot than he has."

"Hey!"

Her eyebrow rose as she gazed down at him, hands on her hips. "Truth hurts?"

He actually growled at her. "Get out of here, before the stink bomb accuses us of doing indecent things in here."

Thornton was incredibly, quietly thankful that she hadn't scoffed at that idea outright, bless her heart.

Instead, Lisa just grinned and headed for the door, saying, "Good night, Mr. Calumet," and hearing a long-suffering sigh from behind her.

"How many times have I told you to call me by my first name?"

"And how many times have I told you that's not professional, and therefore, I refuse to do so?"

His, "A million, at least, stubborn woman!" was not particularly gruff.

"Says the equally stubborn man," she teased back.

"Good night, Lisa. Thank you for putting up with this old fool like you do."

"It's truly my pleasure, Mr. Calumet."

As she closed the door, she heard him reply softly, "Liar."

She should save herself the annoyance and go back to her room, where more studying awaited—as always—but *he* was here, and she didn't think she'd ever sleep comfortably when that man was in the house. Although he hadn't said as much to her face—yet—Lisa had a pretty good idea that he'd never really thought much of her, and she could only imagine what he thought about the fact that she'd actually moved into his father's house.

And she didn't want to go to her room. She hadn't eaten much at dinner—one she'd made for him, since convincing Mr. Calumet that he didn't need to spend the money for a fine French chef when he could no longer eat much of what the man cooked. Rich, heavy sauces, filled with cream and salt and butter, were no longer his friend.

In fact, Lisa had encouraged him to cut the size of his staff dramatically, leaving them with one gardener, a chauffeur, and one housekeeper—because she drew the line there—and he had agreed with her.

She'd been very touched about how he'd handled letting the rest go. He'd winnowed them down, but he had been very careful to retire them with a generous severance package—which was the majority, since most of them had been with him for decades. Or he'd gotten them jobs in another of his concerns, so it was always a lateral move for them, rather than anything detrimental in any way. If they wanted to leave his employ entirely, he'd written them glowing reviews and given them a month's salary, to boot.

Junior's—Hugh's—impending visits always put her off her food, since he did nothing to alleviate the nervousness he caused in her.

So, Lisa decided to rummage in the kitchen, knowing that there were leftovers of tonight's meal—a heart healthy, low sodium chicken and vegetable casserole that she'd made—in the fridge.

Feeling ridiculously like a spy in what she'd been encouraged to feel was her own house, she had to suppress the impulse to look both ways as she came down the elaborate staircase, then she crossed to the door that led to the kitchen.

Minutes later, she had a bowl of happiness warming in the microwave as she poured a glass of ice water for herself, setting it in front of the place she usually used at the bar that was on one side of the enormous kitchen island.

While she debated about whether or not to indulge in something sweet, she heard a slider open and knew what that meant, stiffening immediately out of her formerly relaxed state.

She was going to have company.

Oh, joy, she thought.

Oy vey was more like it.

That was when the man in question rounded the corner into the kitchen, making her rethink how hungry she was, not that she was going to let it show that she wanted to turn tail and flee.

"Doesn't my father feed you?" was his first conversational gambit as he leaned the long length of himself against the door jamb, crossing his feet at the ankle and his arms over his chest.

Lisa drew a deep breath, cautioning herself to be calm. "I wasn't very hungry at dinner."

"Tsk. Don't tell me that my father let you get away without making sure you were a member of the clean plate club?"

There was something in his tone when he said things like that that made her shiver involuntarily. He sounded Dommish, and she wasn't at all sure how she felt about that. Well, she wasn't sure how she felt about it intellectually anyway. Her body was having no such qualms, which was another cause for alarm entirely.

"When he bothered to be there, he never let me leave the

dinner table if there was so much as a speck of food still on my plate."

"A perfectly understandable attitude for someone who didn't get much to eat as a kid."

Hugh frowned, as if that was the first time that correlation had been brought to his attention. "I suppose so."

The ding sounded that her meal was ready, and she brought it to the bar, refusing to allow him to push her out of the kitchen.

She spread a napkin over her lap—something she would never have bothered with if she was alone. Hell, she considered paper towel to be fine linen!

"What is that?" he sniffed.

"It's a chicken casserole, but there's a third of the usual chicken and two-thirds healthy veggies, with a little bit of low fat sour cream, a tiny amount of parmesan cheese and cayenne pepper, and a lot of garlic." Without another word, she got down and made him a bowl, which she put in the microwave. When it was done, she got him a spoon and a napkin then put it in front of the seat next to her at the bar. "Have some."

He was hungry, and it smelled damned good. Food was low on his list of necessities—he only ate when he was hungry.

"Unless you think that peasant food will contaminate your no doubt highly refined palate."

Hugh shrugged out of his jacket, putting it over the back of the stool before taking his place. "I'm not a snob about food."

"Well, that's one thing, anyway. Maybe you're not so bad, but I won't get my hopes up." She was done, having wolfed it down in a manner she knew that Thornton would have hated.

"My, you eat quickly," he commented as he tucked into a big spoonful of the unappealing looking meal—but it tasted damned good. "I'd have heard about that, too."

"I hear about it, too. Your father is trying to break me of that habit. He's not having much luck." She was washing her bowl and spoon, then wiping down the counter as she spoke, not paying him much attention—or so it seemed. The truth was that every nerve in her body was on edge because of him. If he so much as blinked, she knew it, without having seen it. "Besides, it's probably smart for me to eat it before you try to convince me—or come out and just tell me—to get the fuck out."

He let that slide, for the moment, because an errant part of him wondered if he would have any more success at convincing her to eat more slowly, considering how he preferred to encourage his partners to behave, but he couldn't say that to her, of course.

And now he wished he hadn't had that thought as she stood there, obviously nervous around him, yet having made him dinner without having been asked. She was a girl of average looks, but she was downright pretty when she smiled, although that was never at him—it was always at Father.

Hugh's mouth formed a thin line as his gaze lingered on her. No doubt she thought that that was making her points with the old man as she lay in wait. He was quite sure that she was going to try to take advantage of him in some way or other, even if it was just to weasel her way into the will, somehow.

But he did wish she didn't look so cute as she puttered around the kitchen.

And she did cook well—whatever the slop was, it was great, and he ate his almost as quickly as she had hers.

Lisa took his bowl almost as soon as he'd finished, running a damp cloth on the granite countertop in front of him, then washing the bowl and spoon before heading toward the door.

She stopped, unexpectedly, though, and faced him. "If you're going to tell me to get out, I wish you'd do it and get it over with so that I can tell you to go fuck yourself. I'll sleep better if we get that little dance out of the way."

"You talk to my father with that mouth?"

The little termagant had the audacity to look appalled at him calling her out on her use of the vulgarity. "That's what you took away from what I said?"

"One of the things," he answered lazily, turning his seat so that he was facing her.

"Just for your edification, I do my best to curb my language around your father. I respect him, and I don't like to use language like that around him."

"But I'm fair game?"

All she did was smile, and even though it wasn't a pleasant one in the least, it still lit up her face to a degree that made him shift in his chair, casually and strategically arranging the napkin that remained in his lap.

Her, "I didn't say that," was delivered in a low, even tone that his body obviously found incredibly sexy for some reason.

"I do want you out of here," Hugh obliged, "and, when I have to, I don't fight fair. You've been warned." The man was tall enough that when he got off the bar stool, he didn't have to step down very far, unlike her, who had to jump down from a considerable height like a child. He took one step toward her, watching her hand clench the door knob as if it was going to save her from him.

"Go fuck yourself," she answered, disappearing through the door as she did so.

"Good talk!" he yelled after her.

"Fuck off!"

"Again?"

No response.

Then he sighed, realizing he'd done what he'd vowed on the way to the house he wouldn't do. He'd intended to just sit her down and tell her to go, to offer her a generous sum to do so, even, if it came to that, although it rankled him to have to do that.

But—as estranged as they were—he intended to protect his father at all costs from scheming little girls whose breasts would probably fit perfectly into his hands and whose sassiness obviously needed a firm correction—or fifty—square on that beautiful behind of hers.

Damn!

His mind and his body had never rebelled at the same time. Usually, one or the other very important part of his body remained sane enough to keep him out of trouble.

He tapped his finger against his lips.

It was turning out that she was more dangerous than he'd thought. But had to get her away from his father somehow.

2

L isa was surprised to find that he seemed to be avoiding confronting either of them the next day. She had already decided that, come what may, she was just going to continue to do what she always did. She wasn't going to let him disrupt them or their easy, comfortable camaraderie. Thornton had treated her well—better than any other person she'd ever been a CNA for, hell, better than anyone else on the planet—from the start, even though she knew he had been distrustful of her in the beginning.

If she was as rich as he was, she'd probably feel the same way! How did rich people ever know that anyone really liked them and not the size of their bank balances?

At least, being poor, she knew that her friends had stuck around—through thick and thin—because they enjoyed her company. Anyone who had designs on her money was going to be sorely disappointed.

But she thought she'd probably passed all of his tests. She'd passed not just the ones he thought weren't so overt, involving being given the blatant opportunity to rob him or handling his money, but by being there every day, always treating him with respect, and being very careful not to do things or make decisions for him that he could make for himself.

She treated him as an adult and had been horrified to hear that some of those who had been here before her hadn't.

And Mr. Calumet had returned the respect that she had given him a thousand-fold. The occasional off color remark aside, he was the consummate gentleman, down to being not just a little old fashioned and a bit Victorian in his attitudes toward the "fairer sex." She knew that it had long since gotten to the point where he thought of her as the daughter he'd never had, but—besides allowing him to talk her into moving in with him, which she had been against up to the very last moment—she had never allowed him to buy her anything that was more expensive than twenty dollars. She had done so by blushingly confessing to him that she couldn't afford to buy him anything much more expensive than that and handing him back the obviously very expensive bracelet he'd gotten her for her birthday

Lisa had worried that he'd be angry that she wouldn't accept it, but Thornton had thrown back his head and laughed. "I don't need anything from you, Lisa love, besides your companionship and your wonderful care of me."

"For which you pay me generously."

"Not generously enough, apparently, if you can barely afford presents."

She'd glared at him. "You know where my money goes."

He'd grabbed her hand and kissed the back of it. "I do, honey, I do. And I wish you'd let me help you with that, but I understand why you won't."

"So, no gold, no diamonds, nothing like that." He'd taken it back graciously and would have gotten her a medic alert bracelet—since she was an asthmatic—but that was more than he'd thought it would be. Apparently letting the people who were working to save your life wasn't cheap, although he had dismissed the less expensive ones because they were so blasted ugly.

Instead, he bought her a gift certificate to the nearest movie theater, because he knew she enjoyed going every once in a while, on her rare off time.

Still, with Hugh around, it wasn't quite what it usually was with just the two of them and Mrs. Hastings, who came in every other day to do the housework, which Lisa was neither paid to do nor had the inclination to take up.

She ignored him as best she could, but it was hard to ignore something—someone—who was that big, and he seemed to enjoy trailing her around, as if he thought he was going to catch her packing away the family silver in a duffle bag.

After breakfast, she helped Thornton into the shallow end of the large pool.

"He gets in and out of the pool? Aren't you just asking for him to slip and break his hip?"

Mr. Calumet—Senior—opened his mouth to shoot back a sizzling reply, but Lisa gave him a look and he closed it again.

"No, sir. He never goes in without me at his side, and he's wearing the best traction water shoes I could find."

Hugh couldn't remember a time that he'd seen his father in the pool—ever. "Does he even know how to swim?" he asked tersely.

"Yes, I do, smarty pants!"

Lisa wondered, considering Thornton's childish tone, if he was going to stick his tongue out at his son, but he didn't.

"And even if he didn't, we're not really going to swim,

we're just going to use the natural resistance of the water to aid in some gentle exercises. The warm water is great on arthritic joins and sore muscles. Also, I used to be a lifeguard, so I could do a water rescue, if I needed to, and I'm also certified in CPR."

"That's quite a list of accomplishments you have there."

His sarcasm bit, but she masked it.

Thornton started to defend her. "Yes, it is, and she—"

"You don't have to say anything, Mr. Calumet. He's right. My piddly-assed little certifications don't add up to a college degree of any kind, much less one from Wharton."

She made him feel small and petty for having pointed that out, and he supposed he deserved as much.

"Of course, in my chosen profession, any degree would be overkill."

"I take it that you didn't go on to higher education after high school, Miss—"

"Hugh!"

"Wheeler. And you are correct, sir." Her tone was carefully neutral, and she refused to look at him. "I had the grades, mostly, but I didn't have the money to pursue a degree."

"Scholarships?" he suggested.

"That's enough, Hugh," his father chided, but he was looking worriedly at Lisa.

"There were other considerations." She finished their careful routine, not bothering to look at him as she approached his father. "Let's get you out of the water—you already drink enough prunes; you don't need to turn into one."

His father blew an impressive Bronx cheer. Hugh thought it was the first one he'd ever heard from him.

"Well, your lung capacity is excellent, not that that has ever been in question."

Thornton fixed Lisa with a scolding look. "One day, missy, you're going to go too far, and I'm going to have to take you over my knee."

Hugh sucked in his breath all of a sudden. That kind of thing could get them sued for sexual harassment, since his father was her employer.

But she just blushed beautifully at that, teasing, "You and whose army, hmmm?"

Hugh shoved his fists into his pockets so that his hard on would be somewhat less obvious, not feeling in the least better about what his father had said to her. He hadn't realized that they engaged in this kind of banter, and he was going to have to have a chat with him about that subject that he wasn't at all looking forward to. Especially since he was feeling like he wanted to be the one to say such things to her. It was a preposterous idea at best, but at least he wasn't her boss.

"Well, when I get my full strength back, you'll have to watch out."

"I'm very sure I will, sir," Lisa came back with, managing to sound only slightly sarcastic.

His father looked rather satisfied with that response, when he absolutely wouldn't have been.

And once they'd toweled off well, he watched her do it again—take his arm to help him as if he was escorting her into a ball.

Hugh stood there, angry and frustrated—in more very unwelcome, highly unexpected ways than one—but also realizing as he watched them shuffle away that his father looked better than he had in a while.

Oh, he was still much smaller and frailer than he ever

had been before the fall that had meant he could no longer live alone, but he looked as if he had gained muscle tone. He knew the old man was doing his physical therapy—he'd seen the bills. His skin looked better, and he looked healthier all around.

And, dammit, he looked downright happy, especially when his eyes settled on Lisa.

Son of a bitch.

This was going to be harder than he'd thought.

HE STAYED with them for a weekend, and it was excruciating for all concerned.

They lived very quietly. When she wasn't directly engaged with caring for Thornton, she was studying. Lisa had never been one for much of a social life, and apparently, Thornton wasn't either, although when she'd asked, he'd said that most of his friends were gone, anyway, which she found terribly sad.

Lisa occasionally went out with friends—the majority of whom were now married with children or, in some cases, divorced with children. She was the only singleton in the group, not that it bothered her—anymore, anyway.

When she was still in her tiny apartment across town—since there were quite a few staff members living with him at the house if anything happened—things hadn't been much different for her. Get up, go to work, drive to classes, come home, eat something, and study. Nowadays, she had less driving to do but the same obligations. Although, some-times she was driven—by his chauffer, Duck—to and from her classes, if he thought the weather might make it at all dangerous for her to drive herself. She didn't allow it often, but he would sometimes insist, stating that if anything happened to her when he could have prevented it, it would kill him.

Lisa was always incredibly touched when he said and did things like this for her, thanking him profusely, which she was always careful to do any time he went out of his way to be kind to her.

And that was something his son noted while he was there with them. His father was always trying to do things for her, and, to an offer, she'd turned him down. Now, Hugh had no idea if she did that out of his earshot, he supposed, but he saw the checkbook register online—he wasn't sure that his father knew—or remembered—that he could do that. He had to admit that he'd never seen anything he might have thought was any kind of extravagant gift or payment to her.

Even her Christmas bonus was almost absurdly small, probably because his father really didn't know what things cost any more. Fifty dollars wasn't going to go very far for anyone, even a single woman.

Still, he watched her like a hawk, to the point that he could see that she was sometimes shaking, although he dismissed that he might be the cause of it.

Luckily for the three of them, he got a call halfway through Saturday afternoon that sent him scrambling into his room then running out of it, with his suitcase in tow.

"Gotta go. Problem at the Pittsburgh plant." Then he pinned her with a stare, dropping everything into a neat pile, carefully putting his things where his father wouldn't trip on them.

That earned him points in Lisa's eyes—not a lot, granted, but some.

He fixed his dark eyes on her, and she nearly jumped.

"But I have time to talk to you." Hugh addressed his father. "Do you mind if I use your study for a moment to speak to Lisa alone?"

Thornton did not like that idea at all, but what was he going to say? She was a grown woman, as was his son. Still, he felt he couldn't just let it go by without registering a complaint. "I'd rather be present—" he began.

"And I'd rather you not." To Lisa, he commanded, "Follow me, please."

"You don't have to if you don't want to, Lisa," Thornton asserted.

She turned back to him, having already begun to obey Hugh. "I know, but I don't mind. Don't look so worried."

To her surprise, he held the door open for her, or perhaps he was worried that she might change her mind. Regardless, she sat in her usual place in that room, in the corner of the couch.

Hugh stood a few feet away, remaining quiet and just watching her.

If he thought that was going to bother her, he had another thing coming. Lisa sat back as if she was just settling down to watch TV, her eyes lying placidly on him the entire time, too. She'd wait until Hell froze for him to start. *She* hadn't dragged *him* in there. He was going to speak first, or they were going to be in here for a long, long while.

Finally, he came right to the point. "How much do you want to go away and never see my father again?"

"Wow—subtle much?"

"I don't need to be subtle. I'm protecting my father."

"Oh, is *that* what you're doing? And here I thought you were trying to bribe me to leave a sweet, wonderful old man who has become very fond of me and of whom I am very fond in return. I know you think I have some kind of nefarious intent toward your father, but I'm going to state it for the record that I do not, not that I'm naïve enough to think you'll believe me."

There was a long pause, during which he was gazing at the floor, but then he caught her eyes again and said something that stunned her more than anything else he could have said.

He had to change tactics, and he did so quite dramatically.

"I saw your expression when my father threatened to put you over his knee."

Lisa knew that her eyes had flared at what he'd said—it was impossible for her to stop them when she was so startled. But then she schooled them back to what she hoped was a plain, bland expression.

Now, she wasn't sure what to say to him, though. "So?" might be interpreted as too much of an admission. And "You did?" would invite him to say more.

And she didn't want to hear more along those very dangerous lines—certainly not from him, anyway!

But she had to say something, didn't she?

"Oh?"

"Yes." Hugh took a step toward her while carefully remaining a respectful distance away. "I've seen that kind of reaction before, Lisa."

Okay, that was more than enough. So, she decided to go on the offensive, standing up and walking forward, fully expecting him to yield to her.

But he didn't.

Instead, she, who was looking at her feet—anywhere but at him—managed to walk right into him, which she didn't expect. It set her back on her feet, leaning away from him precariously.

Hugh's arm shot out, wrapping around her waist and steadying her, then pulling her just the slightest bit closer to him.

"I'd bet my life that you've been spanked—and not as a child, as an adult."

His velvet covered sandpaper voice was making her wet, on top of the fact that she already felt exposed to him in a way she never had been to any man.

Lisa said nothing. Her eyes were closed and her head was bowed, as if she was praying. As far as she could see, she didn't have much choice, anyway. She definitely wasn't going to look up at him, and if she stared down, she'd be looking at his zipper. And she was praying, for all she was worth, that she wasn't blushing, which she knew he would take as a "yes."

That was until she felt a finger beneath her chin that didn't give her a choice about raising her head.

He chuckled softly at that, murmuring, "Eyes closed, hmmm? I wouldn't have taken you for a coward."

Her eyebrow rose, but her eyes remained shuttered. "Well, since you don't know me very well, Mr. Calumet, being wrong about me shouldn't surprise you. Besides, I'm merely hoping that when I do open them again, you'll be gone."

Hugh had to laugh reluctantly at that. "I noticed you didn't say that I was wrong about you being spanked."

Lisa straightened her back and raised her head a notch, so that her chin was no longer on his finger. "That's because I'm not about to dignify your theory with a response. Please excuse me."

She made as if to move forward, which would have put her on top of him, and, although he paused deliberately for a second, he did eventually yield the floor to her.

"I'm not done with you, Lisa. If you won't accept my money—"

"Your father's money, but go ahead," she corrected smoothly.

His face darkened, and she wondered if she'd poked the bear one too many times.

"—I'll have to come up with another way to assure myself of my father's safety from the likes of you."

Lisa actually laughed. "The likes of me? Did it all of a sudden become nineteen-forty, or what?" She pulled opened the door, saying, "And of course, you will, Mr. Calumet. I wouldn't expect anything less from a heartless bastard such as yourself. I wish you luck in your pursuits."

WHEN SHE'D LEFT, Hugh flopped down on the couch she'd vacated when he should have been on his way to Pittsburgh. A big hand ran itself through his hair as he blew all of the air out of his lungs forcefully, puffing out his lips as he had to force himself to resist the urge to rub the obscenely large bulge that was pressing against his zipper.

Damn, what he wouldn't give to tame that woman himself!

He knew he wasn't wrong about her. He just knew it.

A thought occurred to him and he was up and heading to the family room, where the two of them were. Father was watching what had become one of his favorite TV shows— *The Price is Right*—and he could hear Lisa snickering at him when he tried to guess the cost of groceries in one of the games.

"Stop! You're embarrassing yourself *and* me! Have you ever even been into a grocery store?"

His father looked insulted. "I used to go to the market with my mother."

Lisa looked utterly stunned, sounding much too innocent as she teased, "Wow! They had grocery stores back in the stone age?"

Thornton glared fiercely at her. "Again, you should be very glad that I can't give you the spanking you so richly deserve, brat."

Of course, that was the moment he chose to appear, staring right at her.

This time, she did blush, looking away because she had to or she was going to faint, knowing she'd tipped her hand to him without saying a word.

Now, he'd never let it go.

He was, of course, wearing a shit-eating grin. "I'm departing." He stooped to press a kiss to his father's cheek that was not returned. Hugh stared at Lisa, but she staunchly refused to look at him. "I'll be back as soon as I can."

His father grunted, turning up the volume on his program, and Lisa muttered a distinctly caustic, "Yay," under her breath.

3

When he had left, Thornton turned to Lisa, a speculative look in his eye. Then he leaned over closer to her and whispered conspiratorially, "Wanna do something that will keep you safe from him and drive him crazy at the same time?"

"And what would that be, pray tell? Buy a pine condo? Take a dirt nap? Leave the building?" Now, he looked confused. "Die?"

His frown was quite fierce. "Don't even joke about that. What would I do without you?"

He sounded so touchingly sincere, as if she couldn't be replaced by any one of a zillion CNAs.

Then he came out with, "No, I mean that you should marry me."

Her mouth dropped open and she didn't even know it.

He held up his hand. "I know you think it's a preposterous idea, but hear me out. The first consideration is that my crafty son—who, once he gets an idea between his very expensive dental work, is not going to let go until he's won."

"Like I said before, he gets his stubbornness from you."

"Yeah, well, marrying me would mean there's nothing he could do to get rid of you. I'm completely compos mentis, and I would have no problems proving that in a court of law, if it came to that, although I genuinely don't think it would. You would have my name and any amount of protection that might afford you." Thornton caught her hand, staring into Lisa's eyes. "You would never have to worry about money again. Think about it."

"You know that's never been what I've been about, Mr. Calumet."

He leaned back with an exasperated sigh. "I know. It's annoying as hell. Why couldn't you be the opportunist he thinks you are? It certainly would make things easier on me!"

Damn, he loved making this woman laugh! It had been a long time since he'd ever even cared to try, but he did with her, loving the sound of it tinkling into his old ears, making him feel young again.

Then he said something that made her eyes bug. "And before you go there, I would, of course, be making absolutely no demands of you...in the married way." She could tell how hard it was for him to discuss such things—and it was at least as hard for her to hear it from him! "As much as I tease you occasionally—and, inappropriately, for which I am sorry, but it's one of the few sources of amusement I still have, and I appreciate your willingness not to sue my butt off for it—alas, it's purely false advertising. I am beyond such things nowadays." His eyes narrowed on hers. "You should be very glad that I am as old as I am, though, young lady, or I would give you a run for your money!"

The young woman glared at him. "No, you wouldn't, because you were married to the love of your life! I can't believe you would ever have stepped out on Mrs. Calumet."

He nodded slowly. "I did some things I wasn't proud of in my youth, but you're right. That wasn't one of them. But Martine died when I was still in my mid-fifties and very spry."

"Oh dear! Well, then, I am glad not to have you chasing me around the pool!"

His disapproving look stopped her from going any further. "I would never have been that disgustingly overt and utterly classless, my dear, and I think you know it."

Lisa shook her head, knowing she was going to have to turn him down—gently and politely—in her next sentence, but he preempted her from doing that.

"Don't say no until you've had a chance to think about it and all of the advantages therein, please. We won't talk about it again until Tuesday morning, unless you have further questions you'd like to ask me, and if you say yes, then, I'll make all of the arrangements."

He wasn't sure whether she was horrified or just amazed. "You mean we could be married by the end of the week?"

Thornton looked like he'd been caught stealing the whole cookie jar when he answered slyly, "For you, my dear, and for the chance to put one over on my son like this— which will provide me with the kind of pure, unadulterated joy that I will take to the grave with me, I will move Heaven and Earth to make it so."

She didn't look at all convinced, and frankly, he didn't hold out a lot of hope for her to take him up on his strange suggestion, despite the fact that it was most sincerely offered. Thornton very much liked the idea of giving her what he could—what little she'd allow him to, the stubborn little cuss—while he could, and providing her with a certain amount of safety, both before and after he "bought a pine condo," as she had said.

When Tuesday rolled around, the two of them were at the breakfast table together, which was in a nice nook with a lot of windows that faced the garden, so that there were always nice scents coming in from the flowers. Thornton put his spoon down and asked the question he'd been dreading the answer to since he'd brought it up to her.

"Well? Do you accept my offer? I can hardly call it a proposal, because that, to me, implies romance, and ours would be a purely platonic relationship. But what do you say, Lisa Wheeler? How much would you enjoy sticking it to my son, but good?"

He thought that was probably the best angle to go for. It certainly was among his top motivations to want to go through with it.

"Mr. Calumet—"

His lips came together in an unhappy line. "I think that would be one of my favorite things, if you agree."

She looked puzzled. "What would be?"

"That you would start calling me "Thornton" or "Thorn," rather than that awful Mr. Calumet."

Lisa chuckled, then began, "I can't tell you how flattered I am—"

"I'm going to stop you right there, young lady. Although I appreciate your effort to make it sound as though it is, it isn't. It's practical, pure and simple." He had the grace to look a bit abashed. "Okay, and it's getting my son back a bit for being such a dick, too."

She actually snorted. He didn't generally use that kind of language around her.

"But mostly, it lets me take care of you, which I would very much like to do. Really."

Lisa opened her mouth to turn him down again, but he interrupted her once more.

"Think about it. No worrying about bills any more, no money concerns at all. And you'd be set for life." He gave her the old man equivalent of puppy dog eyes. "Won't you let me take care of you? You do such a good job of taking care of me."

That was playing dirty, and her face let him know that she knew that was exactly what he was doing.

"But isn't this doing exactly what your son is worried we're going to do?" she brought up.

Lisa had never seen such an evil look on her employer's usually cherubic face. He looked as if he should have been wringing his hands like he was some sort of mad scientist. "Yes, exactly."

She decided to let that go. "Well, as much as I'm very much against it in principle, while I was thinking about it, I was kind of drawing up some stipulations in my mind." That simple statement didn't really cover how racked up she had been about this. She hadn't slept in days. Lisa knew what her response should be—an emphatic no, thank you. But she was only human, and she was extremely tempted to marry him, just so that her life would be even the slightest bit easier. She'd never not had to worry about money, and having that stress removed from her life—even for a short time—would be unbelievably freeing.

But that would, essentially, mean that she was exactly the kind of woman his son thought she was. She was in such a tangle about this.

Thornton was amazed she had even entertained the idea. Hearing that made him feel much better about the possibility of actually getting his way in this! Negotiating, he could do. In fact, he was damned good at it. He relaxed in his chair, turning a bit so that he was facing her. He always liked to look the person in the eye when he was trying to bargain them into—or out of—something.

"Tell me what they are."

"Well, you just mentioned one of them. You know how... how emphatic I am about you not giving me things, especially money."

"Yes, you're a very stubborn girl. It seems to be in the air around here. You could already be a Calumet on that basis alone. Go on."

She glared at him but continued. "Well, I still don't want your money."

He surprised her by smiling and shaking his head. "I think you have stubborn down to an art form, Lisa Wheeler."

"Yes, but," she couldn't help blushing a bit, "if we were in love, if we were going to have a full, real relationship as a married couple, then that would be one thing." She grinned. "I'd already be measuring for curtains and ordering Louboutins by the truckload!"

Although he was still grinning, he said, "Somehow I doubt that, but don't let me interrupt you."

Lisa sighed heavily. "But that's not the kind of relationship we can have, so it is less than a true marriage, as far as I'm concerned. Much less." She'd been fiddling with her fingers for a while, and then she looked up at him, finally, saying what she meant clearly and calmly. "Firstly, I wouldn't want you to change your will one bit. No matter how long we remained married, I'm still not really your wife. And, as much as I think he's a jackass—sorry to call your son that and using a vulgar word—" she apologized.

"Come now, aren't you going a bit too easy on him?" he prompted charmingly.

"Yeah, really. But as much as he is one, he'd be right in that I'd be marrying you for your money. I adore you and care about you deeply, Mr. Calumet. But I definitely couldn't feel good about..." she was having a hard time expressing herself. "About being a full financial partner, especially since I couldn't be, anyway, since I bring nothing to the relationship but debt."

"You devalue yourself, Lisa, and I won't have it. You bring much more than that to me every day."

"You're much too nice to say that."

"Balderdash, but go on."

"So, I was thinking that, *if* I did agree, I'd want a pre-nup or whatever is legally necessary to spell that out. I also don't want to be added to any of your accounts or anything. If I need something, I'll ask. I don't want furs or cars or stupid stuff like that. Living here, eating here, having you pay my school fees, if you're willing, that's really all I want. Any or all of that would remove an incredible burden from me and would frankly be more than I deserved."

"Bullshit," he exclaimed, although he was very heartened by the fact that she seemed to be entertaining his suggestion in the least. "Beg pardon. Again, you sell yourself short, my dear, considering everything you do for me. You don't want to have to come to me for every pencil or bauble you want to buy. You should have an allowance of some sort."

She bit her lip hesitantly. "Only wh-while we're married," she strove to put it delicately.

Lisa watched his face set. "You should have some money afterward, though—money of your own, that my son can't touch."

"No. He's your blood, he's your son, and he should have it all. I wouldn't want anything."

He changed tactics, not wanting her to dig her heels in

on that and end the conversation right now. "So, I'm thinking twenty thousand a month." It was more than he was thinking, and he knew that she would balk at it immediately, which she did.

"Hell no! For that amount of money, I'd better be sleeping with you!"

Somehow, he didn't look very happy at that remark, but he recovered quickly. "Fifteen?"

"Absolutely not! That's half of what I used to make at the agency, for crying out loud!"

"Ten?"

She was wiggling in her chair, like a child who had been naughty. "I don't like this. I hate talking about money."

"I know, Lisa love. Why don't we just call it good at five thousand? If you need more, you can always have it."

"More? I can't imagine spending that amount every month! That still sounds like a tremendous amount of money."

Thornton nodded. "It is, and I love you for recognizing that fact. So many people—including my son—wouldn't think it was much at all."

Her eyes pinned his shrewdly. "So, at that amount, I'll pay for my own schooling."

The look he gave her was a glimpse into what he must've been like as a young man, much like his son—damned hard to stare down. "No, you won't. You are entitled to things as my wife that I know you won't avail yourself of, and I insist on paying for any educational—or recreational pursuits— you might want to take up."

"Grrrrr. I can see why you're such a successful business-man, Mr. Calumet."

"Thornton," he corrected firmly, offering her his hand,

wanting to seal the deal while she seemed slightly inclined to it.

She hesitated, staring at his hand as if it was going to bite her, and he wondered if he had miscalculated in his maneuvers.

"W-we haven't settled anything yet. We were just talking."

"Yes, we were talking about settling things, arranging them the way we want them to be. We were talking about what monthly allowance would make you comfortable enough to accept as my wife, so that you wouldn't feel as if you were taking advantage of me."

"Yes."

"And didn't we just agree on five thousand a month?" he asked.

Lisa glared at him, brows drawn darkly, but she was obviously trying not to smile at the same time. "Why do I feel as if I have just been played by a master?"

Thornton moved the hand he still held out to her—palm up—toward her, subtly demanding that she take it.

And, as she did— with a lot more reluctance than he would have preferred, but he wasn't about to push her any further —he grasped it warmly, turning it up so that he could kiss the back of it.

"I promise you won't regret this, Lisa," he vowed, rising to give her a fatherly kiss on the head.

Still not sure she should have agreed to this at all, she replied wryly, "Too late. And you're not the one who's going to have to deal with your son, if you die."

"When," he corrected, having long since come to grips with his own mortality. "And I'll make sure that you're taken care of."

"*No*—that's exactly what I don't want! It's not my inheritance, it's his, and I can see him coming after me for it once you're not around to protect me from him! He's your son. He gets everything." She fixed him with a very intense, no nonsense stare. "I don't want a penny, Thornton, and I mean that literally, or the deal's off."

He was grinning like an idiot for some reason. "Relax. I'll do exactly as you say."

"Then why are you smiling like that?"

"Because you called me Thornton."

She stood, and after she'd gotten a few steps away, Lisa turned back to him, her hands on her hips.

"Hey—I have been neatly maneuvered, haven't I?"

He couldn't even manage not to look obscenely proud of himself, even if his words protested his innocence. "By whom? Little old me?"

"Oh, please! I was so worried about the stink bomb, I forgot that I was dealing with a mushroom full of shit!"

He threw back his head and laughed at that, and it made her smile broadly to see him do that. But when he stopped, he peered out at her from over his old man, wire rimmed glasses. "A deal's a deal, though, and I'm not letting you out of this one, Lisa-soon-to-be-Calumet."

Lisa growled at him again. "Yeah, a deal's a deal."

She walked away, and he had to shake his head in wonder at what had made her so fiercely independent. It was a great thing in some ways, but distinctly not in others.

THE ROOM WAS DARK, and Lisa wanted to turn around as soon as she entered it. The old brick walls, which didn't help alleviate the dimness at all, were the kind that would outlast everyone, including the cockroaches. A big, mahogany and brass bar took up the rest of the same wall as the door, and the entire room, seemed to firmly guide one's eyes to land on the small stage, which was utterly bare except for a microphone stand in one corner and one straight backed chair sat directly—and a bit forebodingly, somehow—in the middle. Lots of comfy looking chairs had been placed in front of the stage, and she was surprised to see that there weren't a lot of them that were empty, even when there was still an hour before the performance.

Not for the first time, she was wondering why she'd allowed her friends to drag her here. There was one friend in particular, whom she'd known since they were both in diapers—Pam—whom she knew had ulterior motives in wanting to come here, because whatever they were going to see somehow involved her particular tastes. They were going to see some kind of a performance, and Lisa was pretty sure she didn't really want to see it.

Pam knew about Lisa's interests. Lisa wasn't exactly sure what she hoped to accomplish by showing her whatever this was, but she knew she wasn't about to give her friend the satisfaction of chickening out.

This was the first time in a long time that she had taken any time off at all. Exams were done, and she'd taken Thornton's not at all subtle hints and decided to take the summer off rather than get more classes under her belt. She'd been working almost every single day since she was of legal age to, and for the past couple of years, if she wasn't working, then she was at school, or doing homework, or writing a paper, or shadowing another friend who was already a CNA.

It was nice to have some time off, although she wasn't at all sure what she was going to end up doing with it! It felt strange not to have something to do besides taking care of Thornton. She felt guilty about having so much free time.

It still felt so strange, too, to think of him that way—by his first name, much less that he was her actual husband! How the hell did that happen? She still couldn't begin to deal with the reality of it, but then, not much about her life had changed, frankly. It wasn't as if they were a real married couple. They hadn't had a ginormous wedding that she would have spent years planning, they didn't go on a honeymoon—although he'd generously offered. She slept in the same room as she had before and did very much the same things as she always had.

Only now, she didn't have to worry about how she was going to come up with her tuition. In fact, she didn't even pay her own bills any more at all! Thornton had insisted, since he had a business manager, that they all just be paid by him. He'd tried to give her another credit card—it was black, and she had a sneaking feeling that it was one of those with no limits, so she had politely declined, much to his displeasure.

So, the money worries that had always been such a sore spot in her life had suddenly gone away. He even insisted on paying that very special, private bill she had that few others knew about—beyond himself and Pam.

But they'd been replaced by what she considered to be a matter of equal—or even more—concern.

Hugh hadn't returned yet, but she had no doubt that he would, and she didn't think she'd dreaded anything more in her life. Just the thought sent a shiver through her body.

"Let's get a drink!" That was always Pam's first thought, even when she wasn't in a bar.

Lisa allowed herself to move with the herd, almost balking at paying fifteen dollars for a Pina colada, until Pam nudged her.

"What are you waiting for? You don't have to worry about what things cost anymore!"

"Shhhhhh!"

She didn't know why, but she hadn't made any kind of major announcement to anyone about her marriage to Thornton. Well, that wasn't exactly true. She knew why. She didn't want her friends to think exactly what she knew they would—that she was fucking an old man for his money.

They had all been disappointed in her when she hadn't been doing so from the time she first started working for him, but that just wasn't who she was.

"He's a nice man, and he's very generous to me, and that is that. I don't want to hear another word about it," she'd told them, in no uncertain terms.

"Fine, but you're wasting a great opportunity. Just sayin'." Shanna was always looking out for number one.

Lisa definitely wasn't in any kind of a hurry to let those vultures know about her arrangement with Thornton. The only one who knew was Pam, and even Pam thought she was selling herself short.

But Lisa wasn't having it.

And now Pam was on the bandwagon a bit, too.

"Fine. You are the weirdest person I know."

"Well, the feeling's mutual," Lisa said, handing a twenty over to the barkeep grudgingly. Good thing it was in a tall glass, because she was damned sure going to nurse this friggin' thing all night rather than pay for another.

Pam watched, though, as she put the change she got back into the tip jar for the bartender.

"I don't understand you at all," she said, shaking her head.

"Isn't that the entire basis of our relationship to date?" Lisa quipped.

They were heading toward the chairs in the same slow motion movement that had gotten them to the bar and were lucky enough to find five chairs all together in a row.

"You are going to love this," Pam promised, shrugging out of her spring coat.

"Uh huh." Skeptical didn't even begin to cover how she was feeling.

"Don't be so disapproving. I've told you that it's the kind of thing you'll like." But Pam had barely hinted a bit at what it was going to be about.

She shifted in her chair, wishing she could do the opposite of Pam. She wanted to pull her coat up and over her, so that no one could recognize her. Why she cared, she would never know, but she did, for some reason.

"I don't know much about what it is, and I don't know if I like the idea of seeing it in public, either, is all."

Pam chuckled. "Public, private—who cares? It's just going to be the same stuff you see on Pornhub, but live."

"You're presupposing that I got to Pornhub."

Her friend gave her a blank look. "Do you like Xvideos, instead?"

"Tsk, no! I don't have time for any of that stuff!"

"You didn't have time for that stuff. You do, this summer! You've got some catching up to do, woman! Jeez, if I go more than a few days, I'm antsy as hell!"

"I think they have medicine for that. Or Raid, whichever works."

Her friend was not amused, but then three people walked out onto the stage, the lights went down, and everyone quieted.

One man took the mic and began speaking, but Lisa's concentration was on the other two people, who a largish man and a small woman. The man took off his suit coat, hanging it over the back of the chair, then set about rolling up his sleeves, so that they were folded neatly to expose his tanned, muscular forearms. When he was finished, and with no preamble, he took hold of the woman's wrist and pulled her over his lap.

She could immediately feel the blush beginning to creep up her neck. Her heart was pounding in her chest, and Lisa wasn't at all sure that she wasn't going to faint. None of the words that the man at the microphone was saying got through to her, because, at first, she was too riveted by what was happening to the girl who was stretched out in that very vulnerable position—one she'd pictured herself in many times before.

Once he'd gotten her there, the man—who was dressed in a beautiful oxford shirt and dress pants—seemed to take his time about laying her bare. The woman reached back repeatedly to try to prevent him from doing that, only to earn herself impressively hard swats for doing so. Each one of those crisp smacks echoed loudly around the room, making Lisa jerk slightly each time, as if she could feel them, too.

First her skirt was folded back—it was a short but not tight skirt, not at all unlike some of those she owned, herself. The entire scene they were playing out was something not unlike those she had played out in her mind on those sadly few occasions when she had allowed herself the freedom to fantasize about this.

Lisa was so closely identifying with the woman on the stage that she began to feel the same kind of apprehension she imagined was building in the woman, even though she'd never experienced it any way but third hand in her life.

Her bottom began to itch, and it was harder and harder

to remain still in her chair, even though it was very well padded.

Then the thought struck her suddenly that perhaps they were so plush so that, if one's bottom had been recently attended to, one could still sit comfortably.

Come to think of it, when she looked around again, some of the chairs the audience were sitting in were the same type as the man was sitting in on stage—plain, old fashioned, wooden straight backed chairs.

They must not be at all pleasant to sit on with a sore behind! she thought errantly, wishing she hadn't.

When she glanced up at the man, he was still in the process of unwrapping his present, but at least she had learned her lesson—albeit the hard way—and wasn't reaching back anymore, even when he began to slowly remove her panties, which he took all the way off, putting them in the front pocket of his pants and leaving her naked from the waist down in front of all of these people.

"Stop squirming!" Pam smacked her shoulder.

"Sorry," Lisa mumbled, sinking further down in her chair and biting her thumbnail in perverse anticipation.

The first sentence from the moderator that she actually was able to translate into her numbed brain was very unwelcome. "As I have told you, Dolly has been very naughty this week, and she is just about ready to be very thoroughly punished by her husband, Levi, who is also her Dom."

Where the paddle he had in his hand came from, she'd never know. It wasn't one of those ginormous ones like frats used, but rather an appropriately sized one for delivering an over the knee spanking.

She guessed.

And as Levi began to bring the paddle down on those creamy white cheeks, Lisa was willing to bet that poor Dolly wouldn't have agreed with her assessment! And she was beginning to reconsider it, too! It only took about five swats before the poor woman was eking and squeaking with every strong smack, her body levering up and down frantically like a see-saw, with his lap as a fulcrum.

Her hands were free, but they had nothing to grasp. Even if she was able to grab onto one of the legs of the chair, the sharpness of the swats would force her to lose her grip and rear up again. Her legs kicked furiously, and everyone could see that she was deliberately bending them from the knee when she did so to try to interrupt—or redirect—the descent of that awful implement.

It was those movements caused Levi to pause for a moment, his hand—and thus the paddle—resting on her already bright red behind.

"Dolly."

Oh, God, his tone!

She hadn't realized that they were both mic'd! It was going to be more than she could stand; she was quite sure of that!

"You know better than to kick up like that, now, don't you?"

That was it. She couldn't stand any more or she was likely to orgasm, loudly, right there in the middle of the audience. Lisa stood up, gathered her coat, and didn't look back even when Pam called to her, hoping against hope that she hadn't left a big wet spot on the chair behind her.

They'd all come in Pam's minivan, but she'd just get an Uber. There wasn't usually much of a wait for one downtown. Since she was looking down at her phone, bringing the app up, Lisa wasn't looking where she was going in her haste to get out of that place.

And, of course, she walked right into some big lug who was standing in the shadows.

He reached out a big paw to steady her, and Lisa looked up, right into his eyes.

Right into Hugh's shocked—then unbearably triumphant—eyes.

4

Those eyes narrowed on her as if he was using them to pin her to a wall. "My, my, my. Who have we here?" he purred.

And damned if it wasn't essentially the same tone as Levi's.

In fact, it was better—deeper, more nuanced.

Definitely more dominant—Jesus, why couldn't he have a voice like Gilbert Gottfried instead of Sam Elliot?

He didn't bother to move out of her way, and he was still holding her wrist, although she no longer needed to be kept from falling.

Lisa quickly realized that it was her left hand, and that wasn't good. She had acquiesced to Thornton and was wearing a plain gold band on her ring finger, which was all she would allow him to give her.

Maybe he wouldn't see it, especially if she could retrieve her hand quickly enough.

But he wasn't about to let her go that easily, of course. He was too titillated at the idea of having found her here.

"Leaving so soon? When she's barely begun to be spanked?"

Dear God, a whimper left her mouth at that, and she knew she was a goner.

So did he.

"Don't you want to stay and watch her dissolve into tears as her husband gives her exactly what she needs? What she craves?" he asked, voice becoming smooth as silk and unyielding as steel. "To be disciplined. To be spanked, when he decides it's necessary? Don't you want to hear her cries, hear her begging him to stop, knowing that he won't until she's learned her lesson?"

"Let me go!"

He did—but not in a manner that would have allowed her to get away without incident.

No, instead, Hugh maintained his hold on her, letting his hand slide down from where he'd caught her just above the elbow, to her forearm, then her wrist. Finally, he squeezed her hand in his, not too hard, but the ring was bigger than it should have been, and it dug into her fingers, making her cry out in pain.

He let go immediately, and without thinking, Lisa brought her fingers to her mouth to soothe them.

Seconds later, too late, she realized what she'd done.

His face drained of color in front of her as he stared at her wedding ring. "You got married?"

She refused to look up at him, trying unsuccessfully to brush past him.

But he caught her arm again and turned her around, sending her crashing against him again, his hands holding her just enough away from him that he could stare down at her, looking ferociously angry.

"Who are you married to, Lisa? Who?" he demanded, and she knew he wasn't going to let her go until she answered him.

Sighing, she forced herself to meet his eyes. "Your father."

She wasn't given much choice about how she got home. The Uber was a fantasy, once she'd told him.

He renewed his hold on her forearm and got them out of the theatre with her stumbling along behind him.

Lisa tried to reclaim her arm, tugging hard, but unable to budge him. "If you won't let go, then stop walking so fucking fast! I can't keep up with you!"

His strides shortened immediately, to her amazement, but he was still holding onto her arm—just short of leaving bruises.

The man knew how to temper his obvious considerable strength; she'd have to admit that.

Now why did she have to think that in conjunction with a man who had hated her on sight?

Soon, she found herself in the back of a limousine. Never having been in one before, she began looking around as she literally sank into the plush leather seat cushions.

"Tell me you two didn't get married."

His tone was sharp, cutting into how she was trying to forget that he was sitting less than five feet away from her. She'd already crammed herself as far as she could physically manage into the corner of the seat, but it didn't seem to help. He may have been a bastard—he *was* a bastard, even his father thought so—but he was undeniably sexy and attractive, too, with every word, even the threatening, frightening ones, stroking her boldly between the legs.

Lisa forced herself to take a deep breath, wishing

Thornton was here to handle him. She wasn't at all sure whether she could manage on her own.

"What do you want me to say?"

She didn't think she'd ever seen any man look more furious than he did at this moment, and she could feel herself beginning to shake.

"I want you to tell me the truth."

Her eyes were fixed, as if in self-defense, staring sightlessly out the window. "Your father and I were married a few days after you left."

Lisa heard his angry expulsion of air from his lungs and felt him moving much too close to her, so that he was practically touching her. She crowded away from him even more, making sure that they weren't touching, although her trembling made that an iffy proposition.

His laugh was utterly humorless. "Let me guess. It was your idea."

Hugh waited for her to reply, but she just continued to look out the window, into the night.

"Did you really think that marrying him was going to get you anything? I might not be able to get to you now, but once he's gone, I'll tie you up in so many legal knots you'll never see a penny from him, and that is a solemn promise."

"Of that, I have absolutely no doubt, Mr. Calumet." She sounded much calmer than she felt by a long shot. No, not calm. Numb.

He sat there for a moment, fists clenching and unclenching spasmodically.

If she had the wisdom of the ages, Lisa still wouldn't have been able to predict where she found herself next.

Before she could say anything—before her mind could even begin to come to grips with the reality of it—she was over his lap, with her wrists caught on her back. His hold was surprisingly gentle but, she discovered a few seconds later, entirely unbreakable at the same time.

"What do you think you're doing, Hugh?" She still sounded relatively calm, for another few seconds, anyway.

"Oh, so I'm Hugh, now? I was Mr. Calumet a few minutes ago. Are we more being more formal now that you're now my stepmother?"

Lisa sighed at that, just laying her forehead down on the buttery leather and murmuring, "Fuck *all* the ducks."

He grinned at that, but it was quite an unnatural thing— as was this entire situation among the three of them. "Should I start calling you Mommy, Lisa?"

"Dear God, please don't," she moaned, not having thought about that horrendous possibility. And of course, now she'd let him know that she hated the idea, so he was sure to continue it.

A muscle in Hugh's jaw jumped, even as his low, gravelly voice came out with the outrageous, "Yeah, I'd much rather hear you call me Daddy."

That got her protesting like nothing else could have, raising her front up off the seat and trying to rescue her arms from his one-handed hold. "Good luck with that, son," she replied sarcastically. "And, if I'm your step-mother, then you have to obey me. So, let me the fuck up."

"I much prefer my scenario to yours, Lisa."

Oh, holy crap, so did she, but she wasn't about to let on to him about it.

"I'm not kidding, Hugh. Let. Me. Up." It came out slow and measured, at least until she felt frantic enough to add, "This minute!"

"I don't think so. My father's not here to help you, and I think that you and I have a lot in common, hmmm, stepmother dearest, considering where we both were this evening."

Lisa suddenly stilled. "Were you following me?"

Hugh snorted. "Egotistical much? No, I wasn't."

She wasn't about to explain to him that her question had nothing to do with her ego, but that she was more looking for another—a more acceptable reason—for him to have been at that particular type of performance, too.

"You know what I like—that I would enjoy that kind of display. But finding you there, well, that's just the ammunition I need, as well as being quite titillating on a whole other level."

Lisa knew she shouldn't respond to him, shouldn't give him the satisfaction of explaining herself, but she couldn't seem to stop the words from pouring out of her mouth. "I was there with a group of friends who decided to go there tonight."

"I would bet you didn't protest about it very much, though, did you?" he asked, his enormous hand finding her bottom over jeans she heartily wished weren't quite so blasted worn! They might as well be sweat pants, considering how soft and clingy the denim now was, threadbare in some places, although luckily not there. "You just went along with the crowd to an exhibition of discipline, of spanking?"

"Something like that," she got out reluctantly. "You were there by yourself, I might remind you! And take your paw off my ass!"

He ignored those last bits because he wanted to. "Oh, I'm sure that's exactly what happened."

Sarcasm noted, she said to herself.

"Does my father know you're here, Mrs. Calumet?"

She stilled. That was the first time she'd heard anyone

refer to her using that title, and it gave her pause, especially to hear it from him in such a thoroughly disgusted tone.

"I don't have to explain myself to you, Hugh."

"I can tell you feel that way, because you're doing a shit job of it. But I want to know what you told my father you were doing this evening. Somehow, I doubt it was that you were going to watch a pretty young girl get her bottom smacked in a public performance. Perhaps you need some of the same kind of persuasion that the girl on the stage found herself on the receiving end of, hmm?"

"Get your hand off my ass!" she ordered more desperately.

"All right." He did exactly as she'd asked.

That was much too easy, her mind alerted her seconds before it came back down again, with considerable strength, spanking most of her butt all at once. He might as well have taken down her jeans, for all of the protection they granted her, although she was very grateful that he hadn't.

She clenched her teeth tightly against a groan that wanted out. That effing hurt! But she resolved that she was not going to do that, no matter what.

He'd get too much enjoyment out of it if he did.

"Answer me, step mommy." How did he make that name sound so icky and so sexy at the same time? And then he out and out threatened, "If you don't, I'll make you wish you had."

That low, rumbled threat careened through her body, setting her to trembling again, lighting fires she didn't want lit in her most intimate places, but settling where she least wanted it—where she was the most vulnerable, where it always seemed to, damn him. His words were so strong, so powerful that it made her hope that the material at the crotch of her jeans was more plentiful that her butt, or her body, was going to make her gush right through it.

Lisa was trembling, and Hugh recognized that part of that was fear, for which he felt more than a considerable twinge of guilt. He didn't like her, and he was never going to trust her, but inspiring actual fear in someone was a new—and uncomfortable—idea.

The partners that he'd played with—or become involved in disciplinary relationships with, which he didn't consider to be play—had all consented long before they'd gotten to this point.

And he hadn't necessarily ever intended to get here with her, either. Hell, he was actively trying to get rid of her, and yet, here she was, over his lap! He hoped to hell that his instincts were right, or he was going to have a lot more to worry about than just the mess his father had gotten into with her!

But he was pretty sure that his assessment of how she felt about spanking was pretty dead on, and finding her there—at a place he occasionally frequented when he was in town—had only cemented that idea in his head.

As was the fact that she really wasn't protesting all that much—nowhere near as much as he would imagine someone who had absolutely no interest in spanking would when they found themselves over someone's knee. And she'd already been on the receiving end of a hand that had been most flatteringly compared to a paddle by more than one woman who had known of what she spoke!

Still, he cracked it down on one of the cutest bottoms he'd ever seen, feeling the soft jeans material, then how her firm curves first cringed away from the swat, then sprang back up—wobbling just a bit in reaction to it—as he moved his hand away in preparation for the next one.

And she was taking it amazingly well. He'd had to put his arm around her waist to hold her still, but that wasn't unexpected. In his humble experience, when a woman was getting a good, firm punishment, she pretty much had to move around. Hugh understood that it was probably quite impossible for her not to.

Lisa, of course, was more actively trying to escape than any woman he'd ever spanked before, so he had to be sterner with her than he might have—especially for her first spanking from him. She tried to lurch in one direction and then the other, tried to scrunch down, through the circle of his arm, or pull up out of it, kicking enthusiastically the entire time but not wasting her breath protesting each spank. She paused when he smacked her, stiffening, and he knew she was fighting against the need to moan or scream. Then she'd resume wiggling and kicking.

So far, she hadn't hit his hand, but he had no doubt she would.

Crimping his arm a bit more tightly around her middle kept her from moving much as he brought his hand down over every inch of her then back around again. But those feet, in their high tops, were going to smack against his hand any time now.

And he couldn't have that.

"Lisa, you know better than to kick up like that, now, don't you?"

Son of a—those were the exact words Levi had said to Dolly as he spanked her!

And they were a million times more effective coming from him!

She knew some of that was her highly arousing position, but he had such a natural command of his voice and tone that it was almost frightening, the effect it had on her! Her body really wanted to obey him, and she could feel her will to resist him physically dwindling. But her mind—however passion soaked it was—was still fighting against him, which was why she continued to try to hit his hand, no matter how much she had to contort herself to do that.

There was no second warning from him, and somehow that didn't surprise her.

As he spoke, a big leg moved up and over hers, as if they weren't flailing away wildly, only to come down across the backs of her thighs and calves, in just the right position to keep her from being able to move them at all. "I'm sorry to have to do this, Lisa, but you could hurt yourself—and you could definitely hurt me—kicking like that." Then he had the audacity to pat her seared backside. "Isn't it better to have the choice taken away from you, so that you don't get into further trouble?"

Dear God, yes, it was! Her body was singing to be so confined by him!

But she clamped her mouth shut even more tightly against saying that.

"Because if you had managed to hit my hand, I would have had to take off my belt. And believe me, you do not want that."

She did believe him! The hand spanking was way worse than she had anticipated, and getting the belt from him didn't warrant ever thinking about!

Just as he was raising his hand again, the car stopped. Lisa didn't give him a chance to say or do anything. This time, when she tried to get away, he let her, however reluctantly, and she was out of the car in a flash, leaving him sitting there. Bill, his chauffeur, at first watched her run away as if she was terrified and then peered back at him expectantly.

When he got out of the car, himself, wishing he had a napkin to hide the obvious evidence of his arousal, he told Bill gruffly, "Don't wait for me. If I need you, I'll call you."

"Yes, sir, Mr. Calumet."

When Hugh made it into the family room, where his father was—flanked by a nursing assistant who had come in just for the evening, so that Lisa could go out—she had already apparently flown by him.

And his father looked troubled about it.

"Did you and Lisa come home at the same time? She didn't even kiss me goodnight! Ran by me like someone had lit a fire under her ass."

Hugh had to school himself into giving a very neutral reply to that. "Yes, I saw her when she was out and brought her home."

The narrow look he got from his father made him feel even more uncomfortable. "So, you've already talked?"

"Yes, Father, we did—and she told me something I really hope that you'll tell me was a complete and utter lie."

Instead, Thornton proceeded to confirm his son's greatest fear. And he did so with great pride—both in the woman he had married, however surreptitiously, and in the fact that he knew it was going to drive his son crazy.

And Hugh obliged him by exploding in anger.

"Have you gone senile, or what?" He ran his hand through his hair in agitation. Hugh tried again. "This woman has nothing. She's going to bilk us—you," he corrected grudgingly. "And for everything she can! Don't come crying to me when she drives the family into the ground financially! I really thought you were smarter than this, but I can see I'm wrong, which, of course, makes me wonder about how your mental capacity—or lack thereof—is affecting other business decisions."

Hugh was surprised that his father just sat there placidly, staring at him with an extremely annoying half smile on his lips. "What do you have to say for yourself, old man?"

Thornton's brows rose. His son hadn't often taken either that tone with him, nor used such a derogatory term. They might not like each other much, but there had always been a certain respect between them, even if it was mostly one sided.

"Are you quite through with your little tantrum? I've always teased Lisa about spanking her, but I'm beginning to think that you are much more in need of one, considering your recent behavior and attitudes."

Hugh blushed, wishing fervently that he could not, especially since what his father was threatening was something he had already done to his father's wife!

He dragged his hand over his face then put them both on his hips expectantly. "What could you possibly say to me that would make me any happier about this situation, Father, except that you got a pre-nup that locks our—your—money up tightly and keeps it out of her grubby little hands?"

Why was he smiling like that? Hugh wondered. What was he up to?

His father didn't say anything. He just put a folder on the coffee table between them, and he managed to do it smugly, if that was even possible. Hugh picked it up with a sigh, opening it to see that it was, indeed, a pre-nuptial agreement.

And what he read astounded him to the core, to the point that he began to wonder if it was real. But there was his father's signature and that of a lawyer he knew was one of his father's few close remaining friends, as well as a notary, and what he assumed was Lisa's signature.

It had to be some kind of a joke—there was something neither he, nor his father, was seeing about this. It couldn't possibly be what it seemed to be.

No one in their right mind—no one like Lisa—could have signed it, not with the full knowledge what it meant for her. The document he was holding in his hands spelled out several amazingly unusual things that just couldn't be correct. One, that Lisa would not receive any kind of recompense—not so much as a silver dollar—if they divorced, or —more likely—when his father died. Secondly, there was a codicil that stated that, during the course of their marriage, she would receive a five-thousand-dollar stipend per month, and that her now husband was not allowed to give her any gifts that were valued at more than twenty dollars. There were a few other things stipulated, but those were by far the most stunning.

"I realize that your reaction to her is tainted by your own bad experiences with greedy tramps, but Lisa is not one of them, and this is irrefutable proof thereof. The pre-nup was her idea."

He chuckled. "Then she's nowhere near as smart as you're always telling me she is."

His father frowned, but he continued as if he hadn't spoken. "I didn't want it, but she wouldn't marry me without it. Even her own lawyer begged, very vociferously, her not to sign it, saying she wouldn't get anything 'out of—his words, not hers—the marriage. I thought he was going to have a stroke when she signed it right in front of him!" He couldn't help but laugh at that.

"At first, she refused to take any money from me at all

once we were married. All she wanted from me was a place to live and be safe."

Hugh's face grew dark. "Safe? What's that about?"

Again, his father ignored his interjections. "But I wanted her to have some measure of independence and some form of recompense, frankly, for what she's done and the harder things she will do for me in the future, since I am quite well aware that my loving family is not willing to do those hard things. I offered her twenty thousand a month, at first. She balked, until I talked her down to five."

"Which is what you thought she'd be willing to settle on anyway," he murmured, still staring at the document. Hugh was well aware of his father's negotiation tactics.

Thornton smiled. "Yeah, she's a smart cookie. She caught onto that, too, and was going to say no even to that pittance, but then I reminded her that—even though this is a marriage of convenience, and annoyance, I'm hoping, in your case—it wouldn't be very convenient for her to have to ask me for every little thing she needs or wants. This way, she can pay her own tuition, buy books, clothes, whatever she needs, without having to come begging to me for it. As you can see there, she staunchly refused to be put on mine. She's got her own, she said, and she'd be glad to put me on them, if I wanted. She's not on any of my credit cards—not that I have many—but the one with the tiny limit I gave her to begin with. She has credit card debt, and I wanted to pay it all off, but she was adamant. So, I finagled her around a bit and got her to agree to let me pay off the largest one— which was less than ten thousand dollars—and she'll deal with the rest as she sees fit. With that 5K a month, she could easily pay them off in one month, if she wants, and she might well. She might be poor, but she's not stupid."

Hugh had sunk into the chair across the room from his

father, throwing the folder onto the table near the end of his speech and putting his finger to his lips.

That meant he was thinking, his father recognized. That could be a good or a bad thing.

"You know that I'll keep track of her spending—whatever goes through the account you set up for her for the 5K —that I see all of the bank statements."

Thornton nodded calmly.

"I-I'm going to bring it up, since you did, and I don't mean to cause you any embarrassment, Father—"

Thornton snorted. "I know what you're driving at—of course it's a marriage of convenience! Anything other than that would be obscene, even if I was hale and hearty at this age, and I'm not." He considered the younger man carefully. "But if I was your age, this would be an entirely different conversation."

Hugh was squirming in his seat at the idea of there being anything other than a platonic relationship between his father and Lisa. And he didn't like the idea that it almost sounded as if his father was trying to nudge him in Lisa's direction, which was just too bizarre to think about.

"So, please continue to tell me how she married me for my money, Hugh. Go ahead. I dare you."

The awful thing was that he couldn't—at least not right now. There had to be some kind of catch, though, and he would find it. Hugh couldn't believe that someone who was as poor as this woman was would marry his father purely out of the kindness of her heart.

"I can't, at the moment, but I will find out what it is, believe me, and I'm certain that it will be enough to convince you to divorce her."

"I wouldn't be so sure, if I were you."

Lisa appeared at his elbow, and both men could see clear

evidence that she had been crying. His father rose as soon as he saw her, looking very concerned. "Sweetheart, are you all right?"

Hugh cringed at his father's use of the endearment.

She gave him a patently false smile. "I'm fine, thanks, Thornton. I thought you might want to retire, so I came down to help."

Thornton took his young wife's hand in his, turning to his recalcitrant son. "She came down to help me, Hugh."

"I heard what she said, Father." His tone was jarringly neutral.

"You didn't say or do anything to upset her, did you?" he seized on suddenly, turning to Lisa. "Did Hugh say something nasty to you in any way while he was bringing you home?"

"No, of course not. Hugh is the soul of courtesy every time we're together." She hated lying to her husband, but what was she going to tell him, the truth?

"Liar," Hugh accused under his breath. Lisa ignored it, but Thornton probably didn't hear it, and even if he had, he wouldn't have understood the nuances of it. Her husband just would have thought that it was a continuation of them bitching back and forth at each other, as they had in the past.

Hugh watched them toddle off together, and this time as he did so, their arms were wrapped around each other's waists, and it made him want to rage impotently against that intimacy.

But he couldn't—they were married. He didn't think he'd ever be able to recover from that idea. On top of that, he was happier than he wanted to be at his father's confirmation that there wasn't anything physical going on between them. He was more relieved than he had a right to be about that, too, for reasons he would rather not explore any too closely.

When they disappeared, he got up and made himself a very stiff drink, knowing that it wouldn't come close to matching the stiffness that was tenting his pants, and all of the conflicting emotions he was feeling were making him want to hit something.

Hugh gulped that drink down in two swallows and poured more, although not quite as much, dropping back into the chair to wallow for a moment, before he reached for his phone. He knew a man who could find out anything about anyone, and it looked as if he was going to have need of his services after all.

When he'd finished his third drink, an hour or so later, Hugh turned off the lights and headed upstairs, bounding up them two and three at a time.

Unlike his father, he was more than physically capable —in bed and out.

How was it that a reasonably nice looking girl like Lisa allowed herself to become involved in a sexless marriage when she—apparently—wasn't getting anything else out of it, either? He discounted the allowance, which he agreed with his father was a pittance, considering how wealthy his father was.

What could her angle be? Hugh wondered, musing about it as he moved down the hallway, past what he knew was now her room, then his father's, and was inches from his own—the one he'd used since he was moved out of the nursery, that was still close to his parents'.

But he stopped short before getting there, having heard soft sounds of distress coming from behind Lisa's door.

He retraced his steps as stealthily as he could, leaning his ear against the wood. Those were the unmistakable sounds of tears, and they clawed at his gut in a way no one's ever had, except perhaps his mother's, on the rare occasions when he'd heard her cry.

Against his better judgment, Hugh raised his hand and knocked softly, almost hoping she wouldn't hear.

But he should have remembered that she was a heath care professional, and even though she was now married to her charge, she was just as much on duty now as she had always been in the past. Of course, she heard him—her ears were tuned to just such a thing in case his father needed her in the night.

He could hear her obviously trying to gather herself, sniffling and blowing her nose, as she then asked, the sound of her voice growing louder, "Thornton? Are you okay? Are you having a hard time sleep—"

Lisa opened the door as she was slipping on her robe, not having gotten it done up. She was modestly covered—especially by today's standards—dressed in a pretty little pink nightgown that ended mid-thigh, her robe full on, just not brought together and tied.

Why, then, did she feel as if she was standing before her stepson naked?

He seemed to have that very disconcerting effect on her, and she didn't like it one bit.

They no doubt had been exchanging heated words downstairs about what she and his father had done—something of which she was extremely happy not to be a part. It was purely her duty to—and, frankly, her love of—her husband that had driven her downstairs to help him get to bed.

Meanwhile, she had been in her room—that was bigger than the entire apartment she had been living in before she'd moved in here—having a nervous breakdown and castigating herself about what she had allowed Hugh to do to her. She should never have let him touch her at all, much less in such an inappropriate way, and she had spent some of the evening dry heaving into the toilet because of how badly she was feeling. She and Thornton had been married less than six months, and, as far as she was concerned, she'd already been unfaithful to him.

That kind of dishonorable behavior was not in her nature, but she knew that Hugh wasn't likely to agree with her about that. In fact, he would probably do everything he could to exploit it, to get her out of his father's life, once and for all.

And, deep down, she knew that as much as it had hurt— and it had—she'd enjoyed it entirely too much, too! If he'd backhanded her, that was one thing. She would have gone to Thornton in a heartbeat about that.

But this—this was much too intimate and much too close to the bone for her to feel comfortable doing that. Her conflicted feelings weighed very heavily on her conscience, and seeing him now, like this, wasn't helping.

He was just too close to the type of man she preferred— tall and broad and oozing dominance. He was smart, and when he wanted to be, he could be funny, not that she'd seen much of that.

And now he was standing there in front of her, obviously having taken a drink or two but not drunk, she didn't think.

"Mr. Calumet, what can I do for you?" she asked, knotting her robe properly and crossing her hands over her chest in belated acts of self-protection.

Hugh opened his mouth, intending to say something that was harsh and cruel and would set her straight about what he was going to do to counter her having married his father, but none of that came out.

Instead, he suddenly took a step into her room, cupped her cheek in his big hand and, tilting her head up so that he could cover her lips with his as he very softly, with a terrible finality, closed the door behind him. He'd discombobulated her so badly by kissing her that he didn't think she'd even noticed that he'd locked it, too.

5

At first, despite how she had just been agonizing over her previous behavior, Lisa melted against him and into the kiss. He was unexpectedly gentler than she would have thought he could be, frankly, and it caught her unaware enough that the slightly coaxing —rather than demanding—way he brought her against him felt much too right for her to object.

But then the mind she had lost as he kissed her returned when he very slowly separated his lips from hers.

And, if the remorse she was feeling all on her own hadn't been enough, the slight look of triumph on his face and in his eyes would have done the trick nicely.

Feeling she had to make an unequivocal move, Lisa took a step back from him and did something she'd never done to any man in her life—she slapped him across the face with all of her might.

The tears that hadn't been very far beneath the surface since she'd bolted up there when they got home rose to the surface and spilled down her cheeks as she spoke, becoming more upset and making it harder for her to speak. As it was, she kept her voice low, ending up hissing at him like a spitting cat, because she didn't want to wake Thornton. "Don't you touch me like that ever again! And that goes for what you did to me in the car, too! I am your father's wife! Doesn't that m-mean anything t-to y-you?"

"Are you sleeping with my father?" he asked, and her outrage must've shown on his face. "He told me you're not."

Her blush made her face flame hot, but she kept her eyes on him regardless of her deep embarrassment. "I will not dignify that question with an answer."

"So, I'm guessing he's not lying."

Lisa bit her trembling lower lip to try to get it under control. She knew that showing weakness in front of this man would be a very dangerous thing to do. "You're always accusing me of being underhanded and self-serving, out for anything I can get, but I think that's a case of pot meet kettle. I don't think you have any sense of honor at all."

Hugh just smiled at that, moving further into her room. It was sparsely furnished and didn't look much different from when it had merely been an infrequently used guest room. There were few personal touches and, from what he remembered of it, no personal furniture in the room at all. The bedspread was different, and there was a small photo in a frame on one of her nightstands, but that was it.

He zeroed in on that, picking it up to examine it. It was a man who appeared to be in his mid-twenties or so and who was quite good looking.

"Who is this?"

Lisa lifted her chin. "I don't answer to you, Mr. Calumet. I answer only to my husband."

"Well, I'm sure he'll be interested to find out that his new wife has a picture of another man on her nightstand."

His threat didn't have the kind of effect he was hoping

for. She simply stood there defiantly in the middle of the room.

"Get out. Now!" she whispered hoarsely.

"Not that I'm trying to encourage it, but you can shout if you like. My parents' room is soundproofed, as is mine, because when I took up drums, I insisted on having a kit in my room that should really have been in the music room, well away from everyone's bedroom. After a week or so of no sleep, my father had the soundproofing installed out of self-defense. And, if you've forgotten, he's deaf as a post anyway without his hearing aids, which he never wears, and wouldn't be wearing to sleep, anyway."

Somewhere, in the back of her mind, she remembered something about the soundproofing, which was why Thornton had insisted that she use a one-way monitor, but she'd forgotten about that.

"Fine." She drew a deep breath and screamed, pointing at the door. "*Get out!*"

He came toward her, and she stepped out of his way, but Hugh didn't intend to leave. Instead, when he got there, he turned to face her. "I don't think so. I'm not ready to leave. In case you haven't discovered it yet about my father, he's very old school. He might threaten to spank you in fun, but he can also be a bit of a prude when it comes to women and... shall I say, earthy pursuits? Considering where I found you this evening and what happened between us in the car on the way home, plus the kiss I just gave you—that you didn't bother to try to break off until I ended it—I think I have more than enough ammunition to get what I want."

Her face went from the dusky pink it had settled on most often when in his presence to pasty white at that.

Hugh took a step closer to Lisa, and if she took one back as she wanted to, her back would be against the wall. She was already pretty well cornered because she was an idiot and had allowed herself to be. Lisa hadn't thought she'd have this much trouble getting rid of him.

He was full of surprises—all bad ones.

And now he was going to blackmail her, holding those things over her head to get her to divorce his father.

She swallowed hard, forcing herself to look up at him, straightening her back and drawing a slow breath into her lungs.

Even though she knew she could scream if she wanted to—maybe even should scream, although no one was going to hear her but him—her voice was abnormally low when she spoke, instead.

"You can go fuck yourself, Mr. Calumet. I am not going to divorce your father. And I know you won't believe me, but I didn't marry him because of anything he can give me. In fact, I've tried to make very certain that he hasn't given me very much."

"I know."

That stopped her suddenly for a second. Then she remembered that he'd talked with his father this evening, who had undoubtedly told him everything and enjoyed the process immensely as he did it, too. For some reason, she colored very prettily at that, too.

Hugh had the strangest urge to want to reach out and pull her into his arms for a tight hug, but he couldn't let himself do that.

"Good. Then you know that I am not trying to bilk your father out of his money, in any way, shape, or form. I-I love your father." His looked shocked at that. "In a very platonic way," she continued, staring down at her hands. "He's been nicer to me than pretty much anyone ever in my life, and I intend to care for him until he dies." Then she looked back up at him. "I assume he showed you the pre-nup?"

"Yes, and he said that you insisted on it."

"There. Would a gold-digger do that?"

"A really smart one might—people have been known to refuse gifts at first in order to engender feelings of trust in the person they eventually end up taking every penny from."

Lisa rolled her eyes. "You have a really horrid view of your fellow man."

"Because I've been burned one too many times, and I don't intend to allow my father to be."

That thought really hadn't occurred to her—what his motivations might be—and that was too bad for him, but it wasn't going to make her feel any better toward him now.

"And I have other ways of doing that. No, I've had a change of heart," he announced suddenly, but Lisa couldn't think that that meant anything good for her. "And I'll allow you to remain married to my father, for now, anyway."

Her eyes widened in surprise then narrowed with suspicion, and she really didn't like how he had phrased that, as if he held all the cards. "Why does that not make me feel comforted in the least?"

Hugh smiled, moving toward the end of the bed and saying almost too nicely, "Because you're intelligent enough to realize that it shouldn't."

Then he took his suit coat off and put it over the chair of her mostly empty vanity, moving to remove his cuff links, unbuttoning his cuffs, then beginning to work on the ones down the front of his shirt.

"Wh-what are you doing?" Her voice sounded positively faint.

His smile struck real fear in her heart. "I'm undressing."

All of the breath left her lungs at once, and her mind went with it, to a certain extent.

But she managed to turn toward him, angling herself specifically so that when she stepped back, every once in a while—small steps designed for him not to notice, hopefully—she'd eventually bump into the door and be able to make her escape. Lisa figured that it would probably be good to keep him talking, moving only when he wasn't looking at her, so she asked in a telling whisper, "W-why?"

"Because I intend to make love to you, Lisa. That's why," he stated conversationally, as if he was surprised that she hadn't surmised his intent already.

"N-no, y-you can't mean that." She could barely hear her voice over the sudden, painful thudding of her own heart.

"And why can't I? If you had asked me before I'd seen you in that theatre what I would do if I stumbled on compromising information about you, I would have said that I would have used it to get you out of his life forever." His shirt had joined his jacket, his heavily muscled chest and its sparse covering of hair laid bare to eyes that couldn't seem to tear themselves from it.

His hands were on his belt, and he stopped then to catch her looking at him with a slight smirk. As he slowly undid it, tugging it through the loops, he folded the ends into his palm, looking at it, and then her pointedly.

"I think I'll keep this close at hand, just in case I need to remind you about how I expect you to behave while you're with me."

It ended up curled on her nightstand, after which he picked up the picture he'd remarked about before, staring at it as if he could discern the man's identity by doing so. "Oh, and he's yet another piece of ammunition. You might not be after our money, but you've certainly shown me many ways in which you are high unsuitable as a wife to my father."

Lisa opened her mouth to explain about the picture but then closed it again. He didn't deserve any explanations from her.

She was still making her way toward the door, slowly, when all she wanted to do was sprint to it and out of it. But Hugh wasn't his father—in so many ways it was tragic and laughable. But in the one that was most important to her now: physically. She knew from his father that he was very athletic and went to the gym every day, and damned if his body wasn't showing her that, to an embarrassing degree. Even if she made it out of her room, there was a very good chance that he would be able to catch her before she was able to make it to any semblance of safety.

And her own weak flesh was responding to the sight of him in mortifying ways! Her nipples were peaked, but she hoped the folds of her gown and robe hid those taut buds pretty well. Her face was flushed and she was panting, but then, she was always nervous around him, and there was no reason to think that he'd attribute those reactions to anything other than that.

That her cream was dribbling down the insides of her thighs—now that was something else she had to hope he never found out. But if he was able to make good on his threat, she'd immediately become just that much more vulnerable to him, because he'd know that she was— however perversely—attracted to him.

She couldn't think about that. It wasn't going to happen. It wasn't. Lisa forced herself to try to establish an alternate plan, but the door to the en suite was over in the far corner of the room, by where he was, and she doubted she could get to it before he did, since she had never been able to afford to belong to a gym in her life.

Hugh was back in his previous spot, reaching for the button of his pants, but then he realized that she looked as if she was further away from him than she had been, the minx. And he was right!

So, he began to stride purposely towards her.

Lisa couldn't bear the thought of yielding to him, which she knew she was going to do—betraying her sweet, wonderful husband and everything she believed in—so she turned around and ran for the door.

She thought she might actually make it, flipping the latch on the lock and turning the knob. She'd even gotten it open a bit, until a big hand appeared at just about eye level for her, and as hard as she tried to stop it, he barely had to exert any pressure at all to close it again. Lisa moved with the door, because she refused to give up her possession of the doorknob, as if doing so would mean that he had won.

And, for all intents and purposes, he had.

She closed her eyes and pressed her face against the door, jumping nervously when she heard him flip the lock back into place.

A delicate wrist was cuffed by a large hand with long fingers as he began to walk away from the door without paying her much attention. She could either remain on her feet and follow him or fall down and be dragged. Lisa didn't think he cared much which one she chose.

He stopped at the end of the bed, and suddenly he was working the knot of her robe loose.

"No—please, Mr. Calumet—you don't want to do this! You're better than this!"

His eyebrows found his hairline. "Have you not been

listening to my father for the past year or so, Lisa? According to him, I am most definitely not."

"That's not true! You two are at odds now, but you're still father and son! Doesn't that mean anything to you?"

She sounded uncomfortably sincere, so he used the lapels of her robe to pull her close. Lisa looked deliberately down as soon as she did that, so he kissed the top of her head, putting a finger beneath her chin to get her to lift it, but she stubbornly refused to budge.

"Do you want me to tell my father what I've found out about you? What we've already done?"

She most definitely did not. She knew exactly what he meant about Thornton. He was very old fashioned in some ways, and more than anything else, she did not want to damage his good opinion of her. He was one of the few people in her life who had been friendly and encouraging and supportive, and she didn't think she could bear to see the inevitable disappointment on his face if Hugh went through with his threat.

Instead, she was going to dig herself deeper, but she didn't know how not to.

And it didn't help that her body was only too happy to go along with whatever he might want. It had already had a taste of him as a Dom, and it only wanted more of the same!

Lisa tried to will her eyes to remain dry as they were forced to meet his, but that wasn't going to happen. It was as if trying not to cry only made her cry that much harder.

He didn't seem to mind in the least.

Hugh kissed her through her tears, although on one level he was very touched—and surprised—that she was so concerned about what his father thought of her and not a little amazed that she was knuckling under to him this easily. He would have thought she would have told him to go ahead and tell the old man, then dealt with whatever the fallout was, throwing herself on the old man's mercy, if necessary, and taking whatever she could get out of it as her marriage inevitably crumbled.

It would have been so much easier for her if he had been deliberately hurtful in his actions, if he had ground her mouth painfully beneath his. Instead, he kissed her as if he felt something for her, two hands carefully bracketing her face, tipping it up gently but firmly as she tried to resist and lost, but also being surprisingly careful not to hurt her.

The lips that settled over hers were firm but not yet demanding, kissing her determinedly even though her mouth remained resolutely closed.

That was okay with him for the moment. His body was enjoying the riotous pleasure of being close to hers.

She was made as if to his personal specifications—short and slight, someone he could easily pick up with one arm, if the mood struck him, and toss on to the bed. Her hair was down, like he had never seen it before, and it was a mass of curls and waves that he was dying to feel clinging to his fingers.

He didn't force her to open her mouth but, instead, reached around her to draw her against him suddenly with a tight arm around her waist. And when she gasped because she hadn't been expecting that, he took full advantage, slanting his lips over hers and pressing his tongue between them, then boldly—bravely—past her teeth.

It didn't surprise him when, seconds later, he felt the edges of hers threatening his tongue, which he retracted immediately. Hugh lifted his head just enough to be able to ask her a question in a gruff tone.

"Did you not see me put my belt on your nightstand, Lisa?"

She reared back a far as she could, her wide eyes colliding with his.

He noted that she was no longer crying.

One eyebrow went up. "Is there anything you know about me at this moment that makes you think I wouldn't use it on you if you bit me? Or, indeed, if you merely disobey me?"

"Oh!" Lisa gasped, her eyes flying away from his as if she could no longer tolerate looking into them.

But as shyly as she was behaving, he had felt her full body contraction at his stern words as if he was already inside her.

Startling her again, which he was beginning to see could be to his advantage, he set her away from him, stripping her of her robe in one fluid motion, which he threw in the general direction of her vanity, then reaching down all of a sudden and pulling the hem of her nightgown up and—not over her head.

Lisa had her bent arms clamped firmly to her sides in order to prevent him from doing that.

But that was okay—because having hauled up her gown, he'd revealed her bare backside, and after gathering her to him again, he began to bring his palm down against flesh that had already felt it once this evening.

Her feet began to pound into the carpet immediately. "No—stop—don't do that! Please—no!"

Each swat brought its own exclamation of protest, none of which did he heed.

Swats rang out in the smallish bedroom, bouncing off the walls, until he whispered, "Apologize to me for defying me, Lisa. Put your arms above your head and keep them there if you want this to stop."

She was sobbing—and those were no crocodile tears—

they were as real as any he had been privileged to bring about in a woman.

But she couldn't convince herself to obey him.

So, the spanking continued unabated and at double time, making her dance as best she could, trying to avoid the swats that he made certain were unavoidable. This time, there was no way for her to kick up enough to interrupt anything—not for want of trying, though.

"My, my, my, you must really enjoy being spanked," he commented slyly, a few minutes—and she didn't want to know how many slaps—later. "I think I need to know if I'm right about that.

"*No!*" she screamed, too late. His foot was already between legs that had been moving—wildly and furiously —for a while now, and soon so was his big hand.

It wasn't just between her legs, it was slipping—aided by the presence of an ample amount of slickness—right down the center of her soft seam, easily finding the answer to his question and discovering one of her most intimate secrets.

Lisa thought she was going to faint, then she put her arms up. Sniffling and hiccoughing sobs, she said, her voice much tinier than it ever had been, "You s-said you'd st-stop if I p-put my arms up."

He almost looked sad. "I said I'd stop the spanking, which I've already done. This," he crooked his fingers just slightly against her entrance, making more gush out of her and onto his waiting hand, "this is something entirely different." To her great humiliation, his hand followed the twin trails of her juices most of the way down her thighs, only to come back and cover those very private parts of her again.

She began to put her arms down—intent on trying to move his hand—but she immediately began to receive a few more hearty swats, until they were well up again.

"No, I said to keep them up, especially while I'm touching you, Lisa," he chided, scolding her terribly well. "So that you can't interfere with me. I'll take your gown off when I'm good and ready."

She might be crying, but as he dragged two fingers up her slit, deliberately curving them around and over her clit, he heard a groan he wasn't sure that she knew she'd even made.

Suddenly, all of this teasing was killing him.

He wanted her. Now.

The gown was up and off her in a split second, then she found herself beneath him on her bed. She hadn't even noticed when he'd pulled back the bedspread, but it was the zillion thread count sheets she felt at her back, not the pretty but cheap comforter she'd bought for herself.

And somehow, his hand had remained where it was, brushing over her as if he'd done it a thousand times before, as if he already knew how she would most like him to touch her.

And he was right—depressingly right.

There was no way for Lisa to avoid, or even prepare for, the way he was carefully coaxing her desires to the fore, leaning down to capture a nipple between firm lips. At first, he merely suckled insistently, but then he began very gently razing the edges of his teeth over her with varying amounts of tension, watching her avidly to see what she liked the most.

And she told him, whether she wanted to or not.

Her hands were on his chest, trying—feebly—to push him off her, but he ignored them.

"I wish I thought I could last through the way I want to taste you the first time, but I can't," he breathed, revealing more about how he was feeling toward her than he wanted to, but she was in no mood to really hear anything but the potential threat of him pressing his mouth over what his fingers now worried.

Hugh watched as her head rolled back and forth wildly as he reached down to present the weeping head of his cock to her entrance, never forgetting to continue flicking her nub, even as he began to press himself into her.

Lisa's hands found their way to his shoulders as he took his time claiming her, grabbing onto them as if they were the only solid thing in her world, and they were. Those busy fingers had done their work, and the fight was draining out of her in favor of achieving the ultimate in pleasure—even if it had to be from him.

She wasn't proud of the fact that her body could obviously see well past the heinousness of what he was doing to her to the ecstasy he could bring her, but that was the stark reality of the situation.

When he was fully seated within her, Hugh caught both of the hands that were gripping his shoulders like lifelines and brought them above her head.

"Oh no no no no no, please, please don't!" No amount of tugging could rescue either of her hands from where he held them in the unoccupied one of his, and she became more and more frantic to rescue them the closer she got to orgasming.

"Shhhhhh," he whispered softly. "Am I hurting you?" She wasn't a virgin, but she was very tight, and it was taking everything he had to remain still long enough to make that inquiry.

The question stopped her movements for a moment.

"N-no."

"I won't punish you—this time—as long as you obey me, Lisa." He began to rock experimentally, and she arched violently up into him, letting him find an even deeper home within her.

His efforts resulted in Hugh being gifted with her first uncontrolled groan of arousal, and how it swelled his cock within her nearly brought him off right then and there.

He needed to hear more of that.

So, as he moved, he teased his fingers over her clit—sometimes using the entire length of them in one long sweep, sometimes playing with her with the barest of their tips. Sometimes it was like a sneak attack, where he honed in and brought her to what he thought was probably her edge, only to leave her aching badly. Then he ignored her for a bit, gathering her legs around his waist and dragging himself in and out of her, deliberately making her feel every inch of him leaving her body before he took her again.

She seemed to like being full of him best, so he only did that a couple of times.

"I want you to come, Lisa."

Her head should vehemently back and forth. "No—I don't want to—please don't—please don't make me come!"

Lisa's eyes were closed, which was probably a good thing —she would not have wanted to see the demonic grin on his face.

"I think that's exactly what you want, to be made to come. I think you like every single aspect of what's happening between us—the embarrassment factor, being taken against your will, not being given a choice about coming. I even think you're getting off on the idea that's me. That hating the man who is bringing you to this point is a large part of what's going to put you over. And I'm not going to give you a choice about it, Lisa. Ever. If I want you to come, you will. If I don't, you won't."

He began thrusting more heavily into her, forcing her

legs to open more widely to him, loving the feel of her around him and the little whimpers she was making, always aiming to force her to give him another moan or groan. But she was keeping her mouth clamped very tightly—annoyingly—shut.

"Tonight, I want you to come, and when you do, I want to hear you use my name, Lisa. My first name. If you don't, when I'm through, I'm going to flip you onto your tummy and slash my belt across your backside so many times you won't sit comfortably for a week."

That was it for her, as he'd had a feeling it might be.

But he wasn't at all prepared for the sound of her.

Hugh could feel the forces gathering within her, winding tightly as he was speaking to her in that very particularly dominant, stern, warning voice. She was clamping around him almost enough to stop him from moving, her legs clenching at him, body taut and arched, hips meeting hips every time he drilled into her, until his persistent fingertips forced her into the abyss.

And she screamed—out and out screamed his name.

"Hhhuuuugggggghhhhhhhh! No—please—oh God—Hhhhuuuuggghhh!"

After the first few, it faded a bit, but even as he found his own violent paradise that had him fucking her harder than he ever had any other woman, he continued to manipulate her clit. No amount of her begging would stop him, until that very last orgasm—her eighth, he thought—elicited an actual growl from the back of her throat as he collapsed down on top of her, finally relieving her of the demands of his torturing fingers and letting go of her wrists.

She lay there beneath him, mouth again closed tightly, body stiff and shaking beneath him, eyes squinted shut as if she was in pain, whereas his was utterly boneless.

In fact, Lisa was shaking so hard that he lifted himself up a bit to look down at her. "Are you all right?"

She was barely able to keep herself from pointing out the irony of his question, but she managed to. "Cold," was all she said.

Hugh rolled off her, intending to tuck them beneath the covers and wrap himself around her. Most of the women he'd slept with had said he was some kind of natural furnace, and they had gladly snuggled up against him whenever they were chilly.

He was unprepared for the way she vaulted off the bed as soon as he moved and headed for the bathroom. Seconds later, he heard the shower running, and he lay there for the longest time afterward, listening to her taking a very long shower and waiting for her to come out.

Eventually, once the water had been off for a while, he yelled loudly enough for her to hear easily, "Lisa, there are no locks on the bathroom doors in this house, so I suggest you come out and not make me come in and get you."

She appeared, in a pair of pajamas that were about as sexy as sweats. They were flannel, and they covered her from her neck to her ankles in big, pink and yellow pastel flowers. She ignored the robe that was on the floor by the vanity, instead, going into her closet to pull out a butt ugly, fluffier one that did look much warmer.

He could see from where he was lying that she was still shivering, even more violently than before, unless he missed his guess.

Hugh jumped out of bed and came to her. Her head was bowed, hair up in a towel in that way only women knew how to do.

"Is there something I can do to warm you up?" he asked.

She was not in the least impressed with how solicitous he sounded.

"Yes, you could leave me in peace so that I can go to sleep." She sounded abnormally calm. He'd expected tears and recriminations—hell, he even thought that he deserved them on some levels. But he hadn't counted on this detachment that was so unlike her—or what he thought he knew of her, anyway.

Hugh considered forcing her to endure his presence tonight—damned if he really didn't want to leave her, especially not like this—but he decided against it in the same thought, not wanting to push her too far, too fast.

He gathered all of his things, donning them as he found them, while she waited—obviously anxious—by the door.

Lisa hadn't looked at him once since he'd made her come in a way that he thought was probably pretty hard—at least in his experience. But then, he didn't know her really at all, much less in that very intimate way. Maybe that was only so-so for her.

If that was true, he wasn't about to let it stand, but he sensed that he had pushed her just about as far as he could this evening.

Damn, he really wanted to know things like that—he was a driven man, and he liked to be very sure he was pleasing the woman he was with. But he couldn't imagine that she was going to be forthcoming with details like that, and even if she was, he wasn't of a mind to think that he could trust what she was telling him.

When he was fully dressed, he stood at the door, too.

"Who's here this evening, as far as staff?"

"No one."

Hugh frowned. "Wow, you really did get him to pare

them down, didn't you! Good for you. I've been trying to get him to do that for years now."

Nothing. No reaction whatsoever. She was just shuffling her feet and shaking, as if she couldn't wait to see the back of him.

Although he fought against the impulse, he really wanted to hug her. But he didn't. He couldn't think that she'd welcome that from him, anyway. He felt as if he should say something to her, but he didn't know what would be appropriate in this highly inappropriate situation, so he didn't do that, either.

It seemed it was likely best if he just left, which he did, giving her a kind of awkward smile as he went through the door.

She closed it behind him with surprising calm, but he did hear her lock it.

It was a useless gesture, but she didn't need to know that now.

Hugh waited a few long moments just outside her door, listening for the same kinds of sounds that had caused him to knock on her door in the first place, but there were none.'

He wasn't sure whether or not that was a good thing.

With a sigh and a hesitant step, he found himself looking back at her door until he got to his.

6

His father—and he assumed Lisa, too, whether it was natural for her to do so or not—got up with the birds out of lifelong habit. Hugh was driven, but not quite that much. He naturally awoke around eight thirty, got up and went out for a run without having seen anyone. He didn't know what anyone's schedule was, so he didn't think much of it.

When he got back, his father was sitting in the kitchen. Lying in wait was more like it, though.

"I want to talk to you."

"Can it wait until I've grabbed a shower? I'm sweating like a pig here."

"No, it can't," his father frowned.

"All right." Hugh came to stand near where Thornton was sitting.

"Did you say or do something to Lisa last night to upset her, either before or after the two of you arrived, or after I went up to bed?"

"Why? Did she say something?" he evaded.

The frown deepened alarmingly. "No, Hugh, she didn't

say anything about you. In fact, she didn't say anything to me this morning at all. Usually, she's a little chatterbox about this and that, telling me about what she's got to do and where she's got to go today and what we're going to do together when we get home. My point is that she and I have always had nice, companionable chats over the breakfast table. But not this morning, and the only thing that's different is your presence here." He was downright glaring at his son. "So what happened between the two of you? She's all nervous and jumpy and unhappy looking. I've never seen her like this. She's been depressed around me sometimes, but this is not that."

"Where is she?"

"She's taking classes during the day now. My new part time nurse will be here shortly. You'll approve of this one. It's a man, and I don't like him anywhere near as much as I like Lisa, so you're sure to love him. But I'm not about to tell Lisa that, because I want her to continue her schooling." He pinned his son with his narrow gaze. "And I don't think he has designs on me or my money, but you never can tell."

In his old age, his father had become much more easily distractible than he'd been when he was younger. Sometimes, that worked in Hugh's favor.

"I'll look forward to meeting him," he said, managing to escape to his room without having to delve into what was going on with Lisa that had gotten his father so het up.

She hadn't said a word, he mulled as he showered in a stall that had twenty-four jets of deliciously hot water pouring all over his body. Damn, he had enjoyed last night —but it seemed as if, even though he was quite sure that he had pleasured her, he was alone in that sentiment—not that he could necessarily blame her in feeling that way.

He was tempted to bring himself off in the shower, but

he much preferred to wait until he could be buried deep within her later, which he fully intended.

When Hugh got back downstairs, his father was out by the pool with a man, and introductions were made all around. Paul seemed perfectly nice, but no one would do for his father anymore but Lisa.

"When you're done, Father, there's something in the way of a favor I'd like to ask you, if you have time for a talk."

"We're just about done here," Paul said. "Why don't I help your father get into a comfortable outfit and we'll meet you anywhere you'd like."

"Thank you, Paul. How about your study in a half an hour, Father?"

"All right."

Thornton couldn't imagine what his son wanted to talk about, but he hoped it was to apologize for whatever it was that he'd said or done that had upset Lisa. He'd allowed himself to lose the train of the conversation while they'd been talking before, but he was determined not to do so again.

When they got together, after Thornton was seated in his big, comfy chair and Paul had gone, Hugh got right down to the reason why he wanted to speak to his father.

"The lease is up on my penthouse downtown, and, if it's all right with you, I thought I might come here and live with you two for a little while, just until I find the right place."

His father frowned, which didn't bode well for him agreeing to the favor. "I don't think that's a good idea, Hugh. You and Lisa don't get along, and you have never gotten along, so I can't think that would be a very good idea. I won't have Lisa feeling uncomfortable in her own home."

He smiled in a way that he hoped didn't seem false. "But, Father, this is my house, too. It's the house I grew up in. Are you really going to bar me from coming home for a little while because your new wife and I aren't best buddies? I don't think Mother would like that idea at all."

Hugh knew exactly what to say to his father to get him to do what he wanted him to do—in this situation, at least. Not usually, but this was a very particular set of circumstances, which lent themselves conveniently to a little emotional manipulation that would allow him to get his way.

"Well, I'll have to run it by Lisa before I give you an answer."

His son was still smiling, and that made Thornton even more suspicious than he had been of his strange request. "Go right ahead. I'm sure she'll be fine with it."

His father looked amazed at that pronunciation.

"I think I'm going to head into the office, but, unless you call me and tell me not to, I'm going to come back to my old bedroom tonight—just while I'm looking for a new place, of course."

"Of course," his father said, almost absently as he left the room. "Bullshit," the older man muttered softly under his breath as soon as the door was closed.

Thornton put it to Lisa as soon as she got home from school, not one to be in the habit of dragging out decisions that needed to be made.

She'd become a little bit more like herself, having left the house and mingled with people other than himself and his pain in the ass son and had been smiling a little and bantering back and forth with him until he'd brought this up.

Now her fact looked pinched and pale. "He wants to what?"

"His lease is up on his condo, and he wants to come home—here—to spend some time looking for where he wants to live next. I know you two don't get along very well, but this is his home, and he did grow up here, as he pointed out to me. The bastard even invoked his mother in trying to twist my arm to let him come here."

"Why am I not surprised to hear that?" Lisa said, sotto voce.

"What was that?"

"Nothing." She tried to smile at her husband. Then she cleared her throat, although the words she said next still stuck in it. "Of course, he should live here. Although I have to say that I'm as surprised as you are that he wants to. You and he aren't all that close, either, so he'll be living with two people he doesn't like. Sounds stupid to me, but it's really up to you. It's your house."

He reached over and patted her hand. "It's our house, now, Lisa. And I know," Thornton agreed unhappily. "I wish our relationship was better than it is, but I'm not sure how to fix it."

Lovely, Lisa thought, mulling that horrifying bit of information over in her mind as she brought dinner to the table, ending up eating very little of it herself, especially once her husband announced, "He's going to move in tonight—probably not with all of his stuff; since he doesn't need it here. I bet he'll put that in storage. But he's going to be using his old room. He'll be gone quickly, I think," he added quickly. She was beginning to look like she had before, and he was trying to reassure her. "Like you said, why would he want to live with two people he doesn't really like?"

Thornton spent the next few hours—before he went to bed, which was at eight-thirty or so—trying to cheer her up, but although she would give him a small smile, he could tell that she wasn't at all happy about the idea of his son moving in with them.

"That's it," he said, when she'd gotten him tucked in. "I'm going to call Hugh and tell him that he needs to find another place to stay while he house-hunts."

He was already reaching for his phone, but Lisa couldn't bear the idea of coming between them—it would kill her to have him so close, and she knew that he was going to take every possible advantage of being two doors down from her, but what if this was their only chance at reconciling as father and son? She couldn't put herself in the way of that. It was more important that the two of them might actually become closer than for her to save herself from him.

She and Thornton had spoken at length about both of their screwed-up relations with their families, and he had always sounded so forlorn about the state of his relationship with his son. If they could resolve their issues, they should, and she didn't want to be the wedge that prevented that. She wouldn't be able to live with herself if she was.

And it wasn't as if he wouldn't make up reasons to be there to torture her, anyway, even if she turned him down, which might well be seen by her husband as being churlish.

Lisa sighed. As things were going, she wasn't going to be able to live with herself, anyway, but this might be some way of redeeming herself—however slightly.

"No, absolutely not. It's his house, much more than it's mine. I'm the interloper, not him. He should definitely move in, and maybe the two of you might just start getting along. Who knows? Stranger things have happened."

Her husband gritted his teeth. "It's much more likely that you're going to be put in the role of referee, for which I am eternally sorry, and I should up your allowance because I will have added to your duties."

That got a real smile out of her. He was always trying to

get her to agree to more money; it had become a running gag between them.

"Don't you dare reach for that phone!" Thornton was always threatening to call his lawyer friend and have it drawn up that she would get another five thousand a month, which was ridiculous. She always had plenty left over at the end of the month, and then another was added! She was acquiring quite a chunk of money in her account, and she'd already paid off every bill she had!

She no longer felt as if she was earning the money she got from him—but his son was making up for that, in spades!

He chuckled but leaned back against his pillows again, patting the hand that was on his shoulder as someone knocked on his door, not bothering to be called in.

It was Hugh, of course, and Lisa noticed that he was grinding his teeth like his father did as he stared at them. Luckily, she was the only one who noticed that.

"You are worth your weight in gold, you know," Thornton complimented her warmly, "just because you make me laugh every day."

"I am only too happy to amuse you, sir." She leaned down and kissed him on the forehead, as he did to her frequently. "I'll say goodnight now."

But he caught her hand. "You don't have to go so quickly. You're a member of the family now."

Lisa could see how badly Hugh wanted to roll his eyes at that pronouncement.

"You'll be glad to know, son, that Lisa and I have agreed to let you stay here. Not for long, mind you, but until you find your next place."

Hugh nodded to his father and at her. "Thank you both. I appreciate it. I'll try not to be too much of a bother."

Lisa was now the one fighting not to roll her eyes.

Instead, she patted Thornton's hand, saying, "I'm going to retire, too. I have a lot of studying to do. Good night, Thornton. Good night, Hugh."

"I just came in to find out what you'd decided, and I have some things to do, too." To her horror, he came forward to kiss first, her, on the cheek, and then his father, leaving with her.

When they were alone in the hallway, he asked her sharply as she was trying to slip away to her room. "Where do you think you're going?"

"Where I told you and your father I was going—to my room because I have homework to do."

"That can wait. I want you." He was guiding her to her room, keeping a hand on her waist.

But Lisa couldn't have that. She rooted herself to the floor and said, "No."

Hugh gave her a surprised look. "No?" he repeated back to her in a tone that let her know he was not happy to hear that word from her.

"No. I signed a form that gives me nothing when your father dies. Therefore, getting my nursing degree is the only way for me to ensure that I can have a better life once he's gone. So, I will not allow you and your underhanded tendencies to ruin that for me."

"You could become my mistress, once my father dies," he suggested outrageously.

Lisa laughed so hard she almost began to choke, bending over with it, holding her sides and actually crying. "As if! I will be gone from this place before Thornton's body is even cold."

Those were very cold words that he would never have expected her to utter. His face became hard at that, and Lisa wondered if she'd gone too far with that—even if it was the absolute truth. "Well, in the meantime, I own you, Mrs. Calumet, so I would suggest that you obey me. I'll allow you time to study or do homework or whatever. But you'll have to pay a price, and I will expect you to knock on my door at precisely eleven o'clock. And don't bother wearing anything under your robe that you're not willing to have torn off you the moment you get into my room."

He didn't give her a chance to say anything further to him, but then, what was she going to say?

LISA GOT her homework and studying done, but it wasn't easy. She'd set an alarm on her phone for five of eleven, but she still kept glancing up at it every five minutes, so the time crept along, which only made her just that more nervous.

At quarter to, she called it quits, because she'd just read the same sentence five times in a row.

She thought about not showering, but she couldn't bear that idea, so she took a quick one, drying off and eschewing the usual scent she used—a cheap knockoff of a more expensive one. Lisa certainly wasn't interested in dressing herself up for him in any way. Her face was scrubbed free of makeup, and she donned that awful housecoat he'd seen before, in a small act of defiance, at five of, when her alarm went. It felt strange to wear a robe with nothing beneath it, and it was cruel of him to make her walk even the short length to his room wearing nothing but that.

But then, what else would she expect from him?

There was no sense just pacing around here, getting more and more nervous for the next five minutes, so at about four minutes to eleven, she knocked on his door.

It was opened immediately, and he stepped back to let her in, saying, "You're early. I'm surprised, but pleased."

"Don't flatter yourself, Junior. I'm early for everything." Her tone was deliberately clipped, and Lisa decided to try to do her best to just go with that kind of attitude. It made her feel less vulnerable to him, although she had no illusions about the idea that he was going to put up with it for long from her.

But it would give her a bit of a boost, even if it was artificial.

So, she continued to do the unexpected, removing her robe and turning to stand facing him at the end of his big bed, utterly naked, forcing herself to keep her arms at her side and not cover herself protectively from his greedy gaze. She neither met his eyes nor glued her eyes to the floor, but kept her head held high and stared straight ahead.

Lisa could see that she'd managed to shock him by doing that, so she gave herself a quiet kudo. Regardless of whatever indignities she would inevitably suffer at his hands this evening—and the humiliation she would undoubtedly feel as her body welcomed each one of them—she would have that small triumph to remember with pride.

"Don't call me Junior again. I don't like it. I much prefer Sir."

"Yes, Sir," she responded smoothly.

Hugh came to stand in front of her, fighting off the urge he had given in to last night to throw her on the bed and have his way with her. He'd been thinking about her all day long, having to keep from standing at inopportune moments that would have revealed that he had been sporting a hard on all day because of his memories of her, and the plans he was making for her this evening.

Again, though, the first thing he did to her was to lean

down and kiss her in what appeared to be such an affectionate manner that it disarmed her to a certain extent, even though she knew that he held none for her.

His lips were soft and coaxing and gentle, and she wanted to return the kiss, but she refused to, remaining stock still, as if the kiss had never happened, neither participating nor refusing to do so.

Hugh didn't allow himself to be deterred by her lack of response but let his hands drift down the outside of each arm, all the way to the tip of each finger then back up the soft, sensitive inside. Then he strolled around to positively gape at the utter perfection of her backside—all of it, not just her bottom, but the long, slow sweep of her back, the dips just above her behind, and the backs of her thighs and calves, down to what looked to him—in his size fourteen shoes—to be very tiny feet.

The sharp swat he gave her, just because he wanted to cup her butt cheek, was designed to startle her out of the stoicism she was clinging to—and very much had the desired effect.

Lisa yelped and gasped, lurching a bit forward until his arm looped around her to prevent that, a big, warm hand landing on her lower belly and spreading out there as he continued to grope and squeeze the flesh he'd heated considerably with just that one swat.

Seconds later, he placed another one on its twin, but she was expecting it and was able to suppress her responses.

He smiled to himself, but she couldn't see it as she was facing way from him.

Good. He loved a challenge.

He would see that he drove her to the point that she couldn't control herself in regards to the punishment he was going to give her—he'd make her scream and cry and beg him to stop long before he did.

And then he'd do the same thing with her pleasure, lifting her out of the depths of the pain he had brought to her in order to take her to heights she had yet to ever reach with any other man.

Suddenly, Hugh turned her in his arms, saying but one word, "Kneel."

At first, he thought she was going to balk right then and there, but then she sank to her knees, ignoring the hand he held out to help her, sitting back and looking back up at him, hands folded neatly on her legs, looking entirely too placid for him.

He was still in his shirt and pants, which he reached down to open, moving the layers of fabric aside to reveal his cock.

She hadn't gotten a good look at it last night, and Lisa could have lived happily without ever seeing it, but if this was a very different situation, if they were two different people, she would have said it was magnificent. Impressive, even.

No wonder she'd been sore when she'd gotten up this morning, she thought crrantly.

Hugh took a step toward her, and she rose from where she had been sitting on her heels to take him into her mouth.

When she would have used her hand to hold him, he moved it away, saying quietly, "No hands."

That didn't seem to bother her in the least. Hugh could feel her relax her throat muscles as he cupped the back of her head and neck, pressing her down the length of his cock without pausing, until his balls rested against her chin. And she had accepted him without the slightest of protests.

He withdrew slowly, then took her mouth again and again.

No gagging, no choking, nothing. He could have fucked her like that, and indeed, he desperately wanted to. She didn't just let him use her, but she kept her entire mouth tight around him, and he didn't think the tongue beneath him was ever still. But that wasn't what he had planned for her.

So, after several deep thrusts, during which she remained entirely malleable to him, he dragged himself out of the warm wetness of her mouth, unable to stave off a shudder of pure desire as he did so.

Tucking himself back up, he put his hand out, and she put hers silently into his. When he used it to help her up, she tried to reclaim it. "Ah—ah—ah," he tsked, and she stopped immediately, letting him help her stand.

But seconds later, she found herself with her legs spread wide, bent over at the waist so that she could plant her hands on the luxurious carpet, her bare bottom sticking obscenely out as the perfect target for his nefarious intentions.

"Now, I was of a mind not to spank you this evening, although I know you probably won't believe that. But I spanked you twice yesterday, and I thought I'd just show you tonight that I can make you feel good—very good."

Lisa rolled her eyes. Men who bragged about being good in bed were rarely good in bed, in her experience. Unfortunately for her, he seemed to be the rare exception to that rule, if last night wasn't a fluke, and she had a feeling that it wasn't.

"But then you came in here with a very defiant attitude, calling me Junior, which I do not appreciate. So, you've earned yourself a spanking. And I thought you might enjoy

—well, not necessarily enjoy—but be interested to feel what it's like to be on the receiving end of the very same paddle you saw Levi use on Dolly last night."

No, she did not want to know what that was like! she wanted to scream, but she didn't—just barely.

And there was no more to it than that. He took a position behind her, and before she had really come to grips with the situation, the paddle began to descend and any fantasies she'd had about remaining unaffected by whatever he was going to do to her vanished at the very first stroke.

That thing was evil incarnate, just like the man who was wielding it.

Lisa didn't even think he was using much of his strength at all, if any. He was so big; he didn't really have to! But he was, instead, snapping it down on her just from the wrist, which was plenty bad enough!

And he didn't vary the strength of the swats, either. He didn't need to—they were horrid from the first and grew only more so with repeated applications!

It took an embarrassingly short amount of time before Lisa found it absolutely impossible to remain as quiet as she wanted to. Short, sharp sounds—like the spanks he was landing on her backside—began to leak out first, then, as less and less of the area he was targeting remained pristine, the solid wood began to land on flesh it had already reddened angrily, making the fire he'd started in it a million times worse!

Soon, he'd covered the entirety of her rear end, and then he started yet another tour of it!

Yelps became whimpers, which became cries through tears, which became moans and groans every time thing connected with her beleaguered skin. And then she couldn't help but slowly descend into short, sharp screams.

There was a dark splotch on the carpet beneath her face where her tears had fallen, and she had already opened her mouth to ask him to stop—to beg him to stop.

But then the last smack fell, and she thought she saw him place the implement on the nightstand, like he had with his belt last night. She couldn't be sure of that because she was crying too hard, although she was trying her best to do that quietly, too.

Throughout it all, Lisa had very carefully and consciously remained in position—not wanting to give him any reason to lengthen the punishment. It had been very hard to convince herself to do that, when all she really wanted was to do her best to avoid each and every swat! But she was again surprised when she felt him pick her up and carry her to the bed. Lisa couldn't have been any more shocked when he didn't just throw her on the bed and fall on her as she had expected. Instead, Hugh guided her onto his lap, placing her bottom between his legs so that it would only be in contact with the soft mattress and wrapping her tightly up in his arms, while holding her head to his chest.

She was at a loss. She didn't want to be there, not here, not now, not with him. But still, it felt amazing to have the same man who had paddled her bottom now holding her and soothing her. He was big and warm and annoyingly comforting as he cuddled her forcibly to him, ignoring how stiff and straight she was trying to remain, with only moderate success, especially as time went on and he simply continued to hold her. A strong hand rubbed quietly up and down her bare back, and sometimes he stroked her hair, but Hugh wasn't demanding anything of her at that moment. He seemed to be almost caring—almost human—which naturally confused her, knocking her way off balance.

Eventually, he stretched himself out on the bed, keeping

her clamped to his side, but even then, he didn't try to cop a feel. He just kept her beside him, her still wet cheek on his chest as he sometimes rubbed her arm, sometimes kissed the top of her head.

Hugh could tell she was still crying, and he also knew that she was trying to hide that fact from him. He wished she felt comfortable enough with him to just cry. He'd given her a good paddling, and he knew that some women used that—or sex—as an impetus to let out some of the things they might have had to tamp down in the course of their lives.

"You can cry, you know. You don't need to hold back."

Her snort was so derisive that he didn't encourage her any further along those lines. If she wanted to hold it in, then it was no skin off his nose.

At least, that's what he told himself, anyway.

He continued to hold her for long moments, then he whispered, "Lie on your tummy, Lisa."

Again, she did exactly as he told her to, without complaint, as he moved himself down to the end of the bed.

"Spread your legs wide, bent at the knee, fold your arms on your back, and, unless you'd like some more of the paddle, I suggest you don't move," he ordered sharply.

Before she could finish getting into the position he had prescribed, she was unexpectedly stuffed full of him. The surprise of being so quickly and fully taken caused her to hang her head down, forehead pressed into the mattress, and issue a long, low groan of pure pleasure that she very much wished she could recall.

But then, he was doing the same thing, too.

Christ, she was tight! But she was also wet, he had noticed with not a small sense of pride, or there was no way he would have been able to slide into her like that. In fact, she was gushing around him as he pumped into her!

Hugh reached down and lifted her hips bodily back against him, so that he could delve deeper within her each time. Then he pressed gently down on the small of her back —just beneath her arms—with one hand, which forced her to arch herself up to him, while the other hand caught her throat, his long fingers wrapping around it with every possible care, but not a small amount of possession, either, quietly and effectively trapping her there. If she moved forward, away from him, he would tighten his fingers firmly but gently, and she would effectively choke herself until she stopped trying to get away.

And he highly doubted she'd move back to impale herself on him even further.

Then he moved the hand that had been on her back around to her front, using it to pinch her outer lips together, seeking and finding her nub easily between that soft, puffy flesh and manipulating it furiously but not directly.

He heard her draw in a sudden breath and felt her try to strain away from him. When she began to cough, she learned the very tight limits he had set for her, and she stopped trying to escape.

That little bundle continued to swell as he teased it mercilessly, slowing his own pleasure to reach between her lips to slip his fingers over her almost abrasively.

But she certainly seemed to like it!

It wasn't long before he could feel her excitement building quickly, but at the same time, she was humming something that sounded like just the beginning of the word "no," but she hadn't voiced it completely yet.

Lisa was trying to resist him as best she could.

He refused to allow her to do that, stepping up his efforts

at both ends, beginning to fuck her hard again and slickening his fingers before he began to strum them over that little bud in long, full strokes.

He practically came when she finally gasped loudly, and once the dam broke, she couldn't seem to stop vocalizing in various hisses and groans and the occasional loud, "No!"

But that just made him chuckle softly.

"Come, baby," he whispered, bending his entire body over her, surrounding her with himself.

"No—Hugh—no—please—don't—do—this—to—me!" she panted, even though he could feel that it was on the verge of inevitable for her.

"Oh, yes, Lisa. I want to hear you scream again like you did for me last night. And I want to hear you growl, too."

"Oh—ah—mmm—stop—please—stop—nuh—nuh—
Noooo! Pleeeaassee!

Just as she began to contract around him, he exploded within her with a long, low cry as he jerked into her uncontrollably.

But, even though he was wasted from the strength of his orgasm, he refused to let that one be enough for her, rolling to one side and flipping her onto her back, claiming one leg and prying the other open so that he could get to her again.

"Hugh! *No!*" Her hands came down to stop him, but he made a reach for the paddle, and she acquiesced quickly. Her meek, obviously reluctant, "Please don't paddle me again," gave him half a hard on, despite the odds.

"Hands above your head and keep them there, or I will paddle you, and then I'll give you a dose of the belt."

Lisa nodded, putting her arms up, but that wasn't enough for him.

"What did I tell you to call me, Lisa?"

Her face grew so red, he thought she might faint. "Yes, Sir."

Hugh found himself entranced by her capacity, bringing her off another ten times, until she begged him not to again, and then doing it one more time, just because he could.

As exhausted as he knew he'd made her, she still bounded out of bed as soon as he was done, searching for her robe in their piles of clothes.

"Where do you think you're going?" he barely had enough energy, himself, to ask.

"Back to my room. If I don't sleep, I won't remember anything about what I studied tonight." She gave him a brave glare when he seemed as if he was going to try to countermand what she'd said. "I told you that I won't let you screw up me getting my degree. When Thornton is gone, you'll have the businesses and the house and all of the money. And I need to be able to take care of myself, as I always have. Better than I always have, hopefully," she corrected, tying her robe tightly and heading for the door.

If she hadn't turned him down so brutally before, he would have reiterated his offer for her to become his mistress, but Hugh wasn't about to give her the opportunity to slap him down like that again.

7

"Now, what's gone wrong between you and Lisa?" his father asked him for the millionth time since he'd moved in, and it had only been four months or so. It seemed to be his morning greeting, having long since replaced the more plebian, "Good morning."

Hugh sighed. He'd been particularly hard on her last night, and when he was, she tended to be a bit withdrawn the next morning. In fact, she had been quite different since he'd first begun to hold the information he knew about her over her head. She was definitely more withdrawn and subdued, no matter how she tried to pretend that the things he did to her every evening didn't really affect the rest of her life.

It was obvious that they did, even to his father, who noticed the difference more acutely than he did, of course.

"I don't know. What did she say?"

"At first, she didn't say anything, as is becoming more and more usual for her, and I don't like it. I don't like it one bit!"

"Well, unless you can give me some sort of idea of what

the problem is, how can I solve it?" Hugh pointed out logically.

His father, however, was not impressed. "Well, she ended up in tears when I tried to find that out, and she mentioned something about divorcing me."

Hugh's head shot up with a frown. "Divorcing you? Really?"

"Really. I know I've been more cross lately, what with all of my new medical crap, but I've apologized to her every time I've said something angry within her hearing, and she said it wasn't that, anyway, but she wouldn't say what it was."

"She didn't mean it, I'm sure."

His father looked positively morose at the thought. "I'm not."

Thornton had been having a hard time of it lately. His arthritis was getting worse, as was his macular degeneration, and he was becoming diabetic. Those things, on top of what he'd already been dealing with medically, had combined to make him pretty crotchety with everyone, even his dear Lisa.

"I wish to hell you two would work it out between you, because I always seem to be caught in the middle, and I don't like that one bit, either."

"Yes, Father," Hugh replied dutifully, thinking that they were very definitely working it out between them, just not in the method his father thought they should, of course. It came to his mind that she might divorce him right after she'd gotten her degree, but he dismissed that idea.

The amazing fact was that Hugh had been living with them for four months now, and his opinion about Lisa had done a complete one-eighty, although very grudgingly at first. But he'd seen it with his own eyes, and had to admit—to himself, at least—how devoted she was to his father. So much so that it made him feel bad about the fact that he wasn't anywhere near that loving and caring of him, and he was *his* father.

Hugh had been trying to mend his fences, and luckily, the old man seemed inclined to forgive and forget, too, and they were growing—slowly—closer. It wasn't easy, and tempers flared sometimes—usually about Lisa being unhappy, with his father blaming him for that fact. And he wasn't necessarily wrong about that.

But they were both determined to make it work.

It was still Lisa who got up with him in the mornings, though—more because he thought his father preferred her company to his. She made sure he had a good, nutritious breakfast, then she went to her classes while Paul came in to take her place. He was a very good contrast to Lisa.

Hugh might not have liked her, but he could see that she did a good job with his father—that she actually did the job. Paul spent the majority of his time while he was there either losing—badly—to Thornton at pinochle or hanging around by the pool on his phone. Now, when Thornton called, he always went to him, but Lisa anticipated his father's needs and addressed them before he even knew what they were.

She went from school to her practicals at the hospital, then came home, cooked dinner, saw to every one of his father's needs happily and efficiently, and got up with him in the middle of the night if he needed help getting to the bathroom, which he did, frequently.

And she did it all—mostly—with grace and humor and incredible, obvious warmth and love for her husband, who returned all of that back to her a thousand-fold, even as he began to feel worse and worse.

The more he realized that his father had been right about Lisa all the time, the worse Hugh felt about how he had manipulated the situation between the two of them. But not badly enough to call it off, apparently.

The bottom line was that he wanted her, and he would do damned near anything to have her. She was a perfect sub —kind of like a box of chocolates. He never knew how she was going to act once he came to her room or vice versa. Sometimes, she was very submissive and did exactly what he said without question, carefully doing everything right— not that she didn't end up being thoroughly punished anyway.

But sometimes—the times he liked the best—she was pissed at him and in a snit, and she did everything she could to resist him.

He adored breaking her back down into the darling little sub he knew she could be!

The guilt he felt about their relationship, and the tentative one he was establishing with his father, drove him to try to be a better son overall and to be nicer toward Lisa, too.

Hugh had been trying to relieve her of some of the burden and had suggested that they hire a cook and a night nurse, but she said she wanted to care for him herself. He was inches away from putting his foot down, though, because she seemed exhausted all the time.

She was coming close to graduating, though, finally. Her classes were harder than they ever had been, and she was more stressed by everyone and everything. Even the easy things.

And her covert relationship with Hugh was hardly stress free.

In fact, Hugh had been harder on her than he had ever been lately, too, saying that screaming when he laced his belt across her bottom or when he fitted his mouth over her clit and made her scream in an entirely different way should help her release a lot of stress.

The problem was that he wasn't really wrong about that. When he was particularly stern and strict with her, she slept a lot better and did better on her tests, too. Not that she was about to let him know anything about that.

And the more benign he began to feel toward her—the more his original outright hatred of her began to be replaced by much more tender feelings that he didn't know what to do with—the more often he refused to let her go when he was done with her. Sometimes, Hugh kept her in his bed well into the night, even if just to hold and cuddle her, which Lisa found to be the hardest part of her strange captivity to bear, since she was still quite sure that he didn't like her, and thus the soft caresses and kisses rang false to her.

It had been easier for her to handle their relationship when he was obviously hateful to her. How perverted and twisted was that? she thought. But he was less and less like that, and she was entirely unprepared for that to happen.

When she graduated—in the top five percent of her class—they were both there, although his father was using a walker by then, not just a cane, but Hugh was taking care of him, and gladly. Paul had come along, as a friend of the family and not his father's caregiver.

Thornton had hugged her first thing when she'd come to find them after the ceremony, clutching her diploma as if it was made of gold. Paul hugged her, too, kissing her enthusiastically on the cheek.

Hugh had made as if to offer her his hand to shake, if only for appearance's sake, but then he said, "What the hell!" and hugged her tightly to him, whispering, "I am very, very proud of you."

She squirmed out of his embrace much more quickly than he wanted her to, but he could hardly hold her against her will in front of her husband.

As they went out to dinner at an obscenely expensive restaurant, which he had insisted on being his treat as a graduation present to her, Hugh let their conversation buzz around him. Unexpectedly, he began to explore what he had been slowly realizing over the months now as his attitude towards her—and his father—had changed: that he wanted much more from her than she could probably ever be convinced to give, considering how he had treated her and was still treating her.

But he knew that, if he didn't continue keep her thinking that he was holding something over her head, he'd lose her —and rightfully so. Logically, he couldn't blame her in the least. He was pretty sure he was going to lose her anyway, in the end, but even though he was trying to be a more honorable person than he had been in the past, he still couldn't bring himself to absolve her of an obligation to him that he no longer felt he was owed. And that he knew he hadn't been owed in the first place.

He was horrified to realize that it hadn't been that long ago that he was still trying to break them up, somehow. During one of the many loud discussions he'd had with his father about his wife, Hugh had mentioned the picture of the man that she kept on her nightstand.

Thornton just nodded his head, seeming not surprised in the least at that, but very surprised that his very smart son hadn't realized what he'd just revealed about himself—that he'd been in Lisa's room at some point.

But his father didn't mention that little slip.

Hugh actually snorted in disbelief right in his father's

face. "Really? Nothing to say, Father, about your young wife keeping a picture of another man on her nightstand?"

Thornton frowned darkly. "Don't make it sound like that, because it isn't. And it's not my story to tell, son."

The younger man shook his head in disgust. "Well, whoever he is, you can be damned sure that I'm going to find out everything I can about him." But he made that vow more for himself than for his father.

"I wish you wouldn't."

And it wasn't long before Hugh wished he hadn't, either. That discovery was the beginning of his genuine thaw toward the both of them.

He had always seen all of the expenses that were charged against the family accounts, but his eye had been caught, at one point, by a rather large, monthly one that had coincided—surprise, surprise—with his father's marriage to Lisa. He'd hired a private eye he'd used occasionally before, especially since he'd been taken in twice within the space of a few years by women who were nothing more than what he had always accused Lisa of being, who had dropped a bomb on him that had left him sitting dumbstruck in his chair long after the man had left.

Hugh had thought about bringing it up to her, but then he'd realized that his father was right. It was her story to tell him or not. He didn't even mention to his father that he'd found out her secret, because there was no need to. The old man had obviously had already heard it from the source, when he most definitely hadn't.

He doubted Lisa would ever trust him enough to tell him anything real about herself, and he only had himself to blame for that.

Once she'd graduated, his father seemed to decline

rapidly, as if he had been holding on for that day, when he'd told her how proud he was of her, and once she'd gotten there, he felt as if he didn't need to hold on so tightly anymore.

It was, of course, Lisa who had noticed that he was sleeping more and eating and moving less. He stopped having breakfast with her, then it was dinners with the two of them—even though they were more pleasant affairs now —and pretty soon he wasn't getting out of bed at all.

All of that happened within a matter of a few short months, and before they both knew it, he was telling them that he wanted to speak to each of them individually to tell them goodbye, knowing that he didn't have much time left.

Hugh went in first, and although he saw his father every day and was spending a lot of time at his bedside, reading to him or just talking to him, surprisingly, he was struck by how frail and small he looked, as if the bed was going to swallow him whole.

"Hugh, come give me a hug, my son."

He immediately teared up at that and didn't bother to hide it from his father as he would have only a few months ago.

"I love you, and I am proud of you. I've only begun saying those things to you recently, though, when I should have been saying them to you all your life, and I am so sorry that I let stupid, silly things get in the way of what's really important. Your mother is going to smack me so hard when she sees me!" Thornton laughed, but then he choked a bit, and his son offered him a drink of water, which he took.

Handing the glass back, he continued. "I'm going to ask you to do something now that I don't think you're going to like, but I want you to do it anyway."

Hugh couldn't imagine what that would be.

"I want you to take care of Lisa when I'm gone. You know

how stubborn she can be, but she really needs someone looking out for her, even if she tells you otherwise, and she will."

He was smiling through his tears. "I think I've gotten that idea."

"She's just as stubborn as the rest of the family. But really. Do that for me, please?"

"I'll do my best, Father. And I wanted to tell you something I think you'll be glad of."

Thornton looked surprised. "What's that, son?"

"I want you to know that I no longer think she's trying to get your money or dupe you in any way. In fact, I quite like her."

His father patted his leg. "I'm very glad to hear that."

"I don't think that she's feeling anywhere near as charitable toward me, though."

The older man nodded. "She's always had to fight for everything she's had, and she can be prickly, but she's a very good woman. I consider myself incredibly lucky to have known both your mother and Lisa in my life and to have Lisa with me now." His father amazed him by looking Hugh straight in the eye. "But she needs a younger, stronger man to take her in hand. When I say 'take care of her,' I mean don't hesitate to give her a bit of a smacked bottom, Hugh. She's just the type who needs to be kept in line a bit. Not abuse, of course, never that! But just a loving correction."

Blushing so that even the tips of his ears were neon red, Hugh nodded.

"I love you, son!" Thornton used all of his strength to say it almost as strongly as he might have when he was younger.

"I love you, too, Father!"

They hugged each other tightly, although Hugh was

doing most of the hugging, and Thornton was the first one to pull back, clearing his throat and wiping his eyes.

"Send Lisa in to me, please."

"Of course," Hugh said, leaving the room with tears streaming down his face.

Lisa's wasn't much better as she entered and ran to her husband's side.

"I know I'm messing with your schedule for nursing me, but I had to talk to the two of you." She gripped his hand tightly, sitting down, facing him on the bed. "You're already crying for me, Lisa love. I know it's hard not to, but don't do too much of that, okay? I've had a wonderful life, an incredible first wife, success at my chosen profession, and I have a great son that I think you, in a weird way, helped me forge a better relationship with. Then I've had you, taking exemplary care of me and making me laugh and loving me despite pretty much everything about me, I think."

"Oh, yes, Thornton, yes!" she breathed wetly, kissing his cheek. "I do love you, very dearly!"

"Well, I have a favor to ask of you that I don't think you're going to want to do, but I'm going to ask it anyway."

That made her more than a little wary of what he was going to say. She had been going to say, "Anything—anything at all!" But then she went with the more cautious, "What?"

"Would you take care of Hugh for me, as best you can? I know you don't get along with him all that well, although I think that's gotten better lately, unless I miss my guess." He peered at her questioningly.

Lisa answered reluctantly and with an abundance of caution, "Yes."

"But he's alone in the world, like I used to be, and he could use some looking after."

It was hard for Lisa not to say that he needed looking after about as much as a shark did, but she managed not to.

"I'll try," she promised, wishing she sounded more convincing.

And that Thornton, even in his condition, wasn't so damned discerning. "Really?"

"Yes, I'll try," she promised again, through clenched teeth.

"Thank you, Lisa love."

That was the last time she heard him call her that.

8

It was less than two days later when Thornton Calumet breathed his last, and when he went, he was surrounded by the two people who loved him most in the world—his wife and his son.

Even when a death is expected, even planned for, it's still a horrible, jarring thing. Hugh cried great sobs on his side of the bed, clutching his father's hand and regretting both the loss of his last parent, as well as the shame he was feeling about how he had acted toward him in the years before.

But the woman who inspired the most guilt in him, as well she should, who had so selflessly been of such comfort to his father, had leaned down and kissed the wrinkled hand she still held, then, with a hand over her own face, she made her way out of the room almost immediately after her husband had died.

For several long moments after she'd closed his door behind her, Lisa allowed herself to dissolve into tears at the loss of such a wonderful man, a kind and generous person who had very quietly given her more than any other being on the planet ever had.

But then she forced herself to straighten her back and her clothes—even though they were just jeans and a blouse —and headed to the kitchen.

There, on the marble countertop, she left the credit card he'd given her and the debit card to the account into which her allowance had been being deposited. She'd already opened a new account and had only the amount she felt she was owed to her transferred there. She'd wait a month, just to make sure that her automatic debits got transferred over correctly, then she'd close it. Lisa also left a key ring with the keys to the Mercedes he insisted she drive, since he wasn't any longer, as well as the ones to the front and side doors and any others that pertained to living in this house with him, since she no longer did.

She'd been cleaning out her room covertly for the past few weeks, knowing the end wasn't far off and wanting to be as prepared as possible. It wasn't as if she had much, anyway, besides books, books, and more books, from all of that schooling she'd done, that Thornton's generosity had allowed her to devote herself to finishing.

In memory of her wonderful husband, the only thing she kept from this strange and wonderful episode in her life was the plain, old fashioned gold band that her husband had insisted she wear, joking at the time that he wanted to warn off the young studs from sniffing around his wife.

As if any ever had, but she hadn't said that to him.

The only one who had ever sniffed around her was his very own son, she grimaced as she got into her friend Pam's car. And that fiasco of a situation was now well and truly over.

Pam held out her arms to Lisa for a hug, but even though she was sobbing nearly to the point of retching, all Lisa wanted was to get the hell out of there.

"D-drive!"

Since she'd given up her apartment and had been busy enough taking care of Thornton, she hadn't had a chance to find another one. But—again, thanks to him—she had more than enough money to get a nice one, if she wanted, although her penny pinching ways really hadn't changed, even though she'd been married to a multi-millionaire.

Much to his disgust, she thought, almost smiling through her tears.

HUGH DIDN'T REALIZE that she was gone until he lifted his head and he realized that he and Paul were the only people in the room.

"When did she leave?" he asked, hugging Paul, who was crying, too, as he was.

"A few seconds after your father left us. She kissed his hand, and then she got up and left the room."

"Thank you, Paul. You know who to call?"

Thornton had made all of his own arrangements, of course, and Paul knew which funeral home his father had wanted to use.

"Thank you, man. I'm going to go see if Lisa is all right."

Paul nodded, sniffling.

She wasn't in the hall or her room—he even checked his room, on the very off chance, but of course, she wasn't there, either. Nor was she by the pool, in his father's study—now his, he thought weirdly—or in the kitchen, which was the last place he checked.

That was when he saw the neat little pile she'd made.

There was no note, just a bunch of stuff he'd somehow

never expected—or wanted—to get back, not that she would know that.

She'd left nearly everything in her bedroom, too, except for her nursing books, and she'd spent so much time with them over the past years that he hadn't thought anything of it when they'd began disappearing. He figured she was selling them online or donating them to the college library or something.

But she'd obviously been planning this.

Suddenly, what she'd said to him a while ago came to mind, when she'd laughed at him for suggesting—off the cuff—that she might become his mistress once his father died. It was a warning that he would never have thought to heed.

"I will be gone from this place before Thornton's body is even cold."

And she'd made good on it.

Hugh looked around the house again, wondering if she'd left some kind of clue as to where she was going, but he found nothing, even after he tore her room apart.

"Mr. Calumet?"

Startled, he turned, his hand halfway through his hair in frustration.

"The funeral home people are here."

As much as he very much wanted to solve this mystery, he had other things he had to worry about at the moment.

The funeral itself was already planned, and it wasn't really even that, because his father hated the wake and all of that stuff. He'd written letters to those he thought might be interested in coming and to those he wanted to come, to a party that he'd already arranged long since, to be hosted at the house. He'd already hired the band and the caterers and even paid everyone up front.

All that he'd been waiting for was the date for it, which his son filled in tearfully on every single one of them.

None of them, he'd noticed, were for Lisa. His father must've assumed that she would stay there after he'd died, at least for a little while. And Hugh certainly wished she had, every single second of every single day.

And when that day rolled around, he became chief mourner, because his father's wife—who hardly anyone knew about—wasn't there. He had hopes that she might make an appearance, but she didn't. And he would have seen her if she'd been there, because he was compulsively scanning the crowd, to the point that he thought he'd probably pissed off some of his aunts and cousins by being somewhat inattentive, in favor of catching a glimpse of her.

But there was none.

He held a small graveside service, as he'd promised his father he would and as his father had already arranged, but he didn't expect her to attend that, since she hadn't bothered with the party. There were only a handful of people there—himself, Paul, some of his father's business associates who were still alive and in varying states of bad health, as well as a few of his mother's relatives.

Hugh was having a hard time of it, all of his own making, of course, and he spent most of the short, quiet service with his head bowed, not liking the idea of crying in front of all of these strangers, even though most of them were people he'd known all his life.

When he did finally look up, once it was over, he caught a movement out of the corner of his eye and saw a small, thin figure in a black coat walking away from everyone, toward where the cars were parked.

Again, he pissed off his relatives by dashing away from the receiving line in hot pursuit.

"Lisa!" he called. The woman stumbled, as if startled, but she didn't stop walking. Nor did she speed up, though.

Hugh sprinted easily ahead of her and began walking backward. "It *is* you."

"Yes, it's your former stepmother. Congratu-fucking-lations. Now get out of my way."

He did as she asked but just fell into step beside her.

It was on the tip of his tongue to say something dominant to her, expecting her to obey him, but he knew that would no longer fly, so he settled for the ever lame, "I was worried about you when you left so precipitously after my father died."

"There was nothing there for me any longer, once your father passed."

Hugh nodded. "The will is being read day after tomorrow."

"I'm sure you'll enjoy the ever-loving fuck out of that. You'll have everything you ever wanted in life—everything your father worked for all his life is just going to fall into your lap. Way to inherit everything, Junior. You must be so proud of yourself."

He was taken aback by her vitriol, but then he knew he shouldn't have been.

They were at her car already, and she hit the button on the fob to open it.

He didn't want to let her go, so he wrapped his fingers very gently around her upper arm.

And she clocked him one across his face—hard, and open handed. It sounded like a gunshot and was so loud that the people at the graveside turned to look at them.

When she spoke, he could see that she was shaking with fury. "Take your hands off me, Mr. Calumet. You don't get to inherit me in the will."

Hugh raised his hands and took a step back from her, saying two words to her that she was amazed he even knew. "I'm sorry." He shoved his fists into his pockets. "I know I have no right to touch you. I'm just glad to see you again."

As she got into her car, Lisa ground out, "I can't say the feeling is mutual."

With that, she closed the door, started the car, and left him standing there like an idiot.

Like a lovesick idiot, he finally admitted to himself, who was never, ever going to see the woman for whom he had those new and budding feelings ever again, if she had anything to say about it. And the only honest thing he could do was applaud her for that stance.

Truly.

The reading of the will was a bit of an upset. Leave it to his father to do the unexpected. He'd ignored what both of them wanted. His son had wanted everything, and his wife hadn't wanted anything. So, he'd given his wife the land around his house and his son the actual house—saying that he thought that was pretty equitable. He'd also left her a reasonable chunk of change, too.

Although he'd addressed his son directly in the will, he hadn't done so with his wife, as if he'd known her more than well enough to know that she wasn't going to attend, since she didn't expect to get anything.

He did give her a letter, though, and he wondered if it said the complimentary thing to what his did, which was simply, "Love her if you can."

"Is it all right with you if I bring that to her?" His father's lawyer shrugged. "As long as you know that I'm going to send her a follow up letter telling her that you said that and about what she's inherited."

"Go right ahead."

As much as he'd tried to stop himself from doing so, he'd been keeping tabs on her. Honestly, even though she'd driven her friend's car to the graveside service, it was excruciatingly easy to do. She was staying with Pam, hadn't gotten a job yet, and seemed to be taking some kind of a break, which she heartily deserved.

He'd used a guy he knew, who had tailed her for a week, but he probably could have done it himself.

"Sometimes she doesn't go out at all, sometimes she eats breakfast as Hinkley's Countryside, on Main. Other times, she goes to yoga, sometimes she doesn't. I tell you, boss, she's boring as fuck, this woman. She doesn't go out, and if she does, it's just to the movies. She doesn't see anyone; she doesn't do anything."

"No boyfriends?"

"Not that I saw."

He wasn't worried about the man in the picture anymore, but that didn't mean that there couldn't be someone else in her life.

"What about her friend?"

"Oh, she goes out all the time—so would I, with kids like those! The kids go to the grandparents every weekend, and hubby is usually out of town on business over the weekend, so, wife goes out Friday and Saturday nights."

"She doesn't go with her?"

He shook his head. "I watched her all weekend. She stayed home."

It was Friday, so he knew that Lisa would be there, and he arrived—on purpose—just about dinnertime, and what he hoped would happen did.

Pam's place was a middle-class ranch in a reasonably good subdivision that was hopping with delivery cars. He'd dressed down, just in case, in jeans and a golf shirt.

Hugh rang the doorbell and heard her call, "I'll be right there!"

When she opened the door and saw who it was, she tried to close it again.

"Don't you want your pizza?" he asked, while putting his foot between the door and the doorframe at the same time.

"Not if the price for it is having to spend any time with you, no." Lisa glanced down. "And get your fat foot out of the way of the door."

"No. The will was read today, and I have some stuff for you that you need to sign,"

It was a lie—his father's lawyer had that stuff—but if it would get her to talk to him, it was worth it, and he'd apologize profusely to her later. If she found out and called him on it. He gave it a fifty-fifty chance that she'd call him on it.

She stood there for a moment, looking him up and down, then she drew a deep breath and sighed it out loudly, turning away from the door to head back into the house.

If he followed her in, he followed her in. She didn't really care one way or the other.

She'd established a nest for herself in one corner of Pam's big sectional. At a quick glance, he could see that there was a bag of chips next to her, as well as one of Skittles Original flavor, and a fifth of cherry vodka that was down at least a quart.

He hadn't expected this. She had eaten so healthily around his father that he had kind of assumed that she didn't eat junk food or drink booze at all, save for that one Pina colada at the club that had betrayed them to each other.

He put the pizza on the coffee table then withdrew to stand behind the couch. "Aren't you going to offer me something?"

Lisa's eyes raked over him indolently. "No, but I'll give you a boot in the ass, if you don't come to your point in about five seconds and then get the fuck out of here in ten."

He tried not to show his surprise at her attitude, but he didn't think he was managing to conceal it at all.

And Lisa didn't care. She'd had a bit of a breakdown after Thornton had died. She'd never had one before in her life—she couldn't have afforded to even if she needed to—but she'd moved in with Pam and just wallowed. She cried at inopportune moments, she barely left the couch except when Pam nagged her to get up and go out and do something, which usually just ended up with her pretending to go to yoga while eating at one of her favorite family owned places on Main Street instead.

She was so different from her usual self that Pam had made her promise to go see a doctor next week to get some antidepressants "or something."

Lisa figured that meant that she was rapidly wearing out her welcome, but she cooked for Pam's brood, when the mood struck, and she figured that was a reasonable trade.

She intended to start getting her decimated life back together soon—probably after she started taking the drugs.

"So, I get that you don't want to see me for any longer than you absolutely have to."

"*Bingo*, Junior!"

He gave her a very dominant look at that, but she merely smiled.

"That shit doesn't work on me anymore, Junior."

In self-defense—to keep himself from taking her over his knee—he handed her the letter, which distracted her.

"Open that later. Father ignored what either of us wanted and did what he wanted, which shouldn't surprise us in the least. He gave me the house—he said something about you wanting me to have the house that I grew up in, so you refused to take the house."

"Damn straight."

"Yeah, but what he did, instead, was to give you the land on which it sits. As well as a pretty hefty chunk of money."

Lisa groaned loudly. "Your father could be a real pain in the ass."

"Yeah, he could."

"He was nowhere near your caliber, though."

To her surprise, Hugh nodded at that. "Agreed."

"Stop being cooperative. It's freaking me out." She fixed her gaze on him, realizing, not for the first time, what a hunk he was. Too bad he was such a dick. "Anything else, Junior?"

Hugh clenched his fists and counted to ten. "You had better be damned glad that you're not mine any more, Lisa. Because if you were, you wouldn't be sitting down for any reason voluntarily for at least a month."

She smiled slyly. "But I'm not, Junior, and I never will be again." That muscle jumping in his jaw would have made her heart thud against her ribs a month ago. She ignored the fact that it was doing that right now in favor of saying, "Leave whatever paperwork you have on the table in the foyer and get out of here."

To her great surprise, and not a little disappointment, he did exactly as she told him to. But then he reappeared.

"You again?"

"Yeah, me again. I forgot to tell you that my father also allotted for your brother—Ben, I believe, the man in the picture on your nightstand—to have his care paid for until his death."

That wasn't quite true, either. He was doing that himself, figuring it was the least he could do for her, considering what he'd done to her. And it just saved arguing with her about it if he used his father's name in vain.

"It's a done deal—nothing you have to do about that. He's paid them well ahead."

That sobered her right up. "Y-you know about Benny?"

She sounded more delicate in that moment than he'd heard her in a while, and he saw her eyes fill with tears.

Hugh nodded, wanting to hug her, but knowing he couldn't. "For a while now. He'll be well taken care of for the rest of his life at Longwood's, I promise."

She nodded, still crying, her head bowed, a hand over her face as if she didn't want him to see her crying. That, of course, was patently ridiculous, since he'd seen her cry plenty—hell, he'd been the cause of her doing a lot more than just crying.

He sighed, stepping away and heading back through the door.

Just as he opened it, he heard her say, "Junior?"

"Yes, Lisa?"

"Thank you for bringing that stuff over to me."

"You're welcome. Is there anything I could do for you?"

She was suspicious of him being solicitous, because that was so different from her usual experience of him. "Go away. I never want to see you again."

Hugh gripped the doorknob fit to break it at that, nodding his head jerkily as he tried to deal with a pain that was exponentially worse than losing his father.

Because he understood her attitude towards him. He did. And he knew beyond a shadow of a doubt that it was nothing more than he deserved.

"Right. Take care, Lisa."

He closed the door before he could hear whether she'd said anything else after that, and he'd made his way to his car purely by dumb luck, because he couldn't see through the tears that had pooled in his eyes.

Behind him, Lisa, too, was crying as she opened the letter from her dead husband.

It was only one line long, but it hit its mark, and she had to put it away from her, staring at it for a long time as if it was a snake.

"Love him if you can."

WHEN ALL WAS SAID and done in regards to his father, Hugh threw himself into work.

"When is my next meeting, and who is it with, Riley, do you remember?" He was trying to sort through a million spreadsheets worth of information, and his phone was across the room at the moment, where he had forgotten it after his last meeting.

"Yes, it's at ten-fifteen, and it's with..."

There was a long pause that was highly unusual for Riley. Usually, he was on top of everything.

"Out with it, man. Who's it with?"

"Well, I'm just going to read the entry to you: your former stepmother?"

Hugh's head snapped up so quickly and so hard that he hurt himself.

"Jesus, does it really say that?"

"Yes."

"Fuck! Clear my calendar for the day, please."

"But you have—"

Riley appeared in the doorway, but the look he got from his boss sent him scampering back to his desk with a hasty, "Yes, sir."

It was ten now, and he knew that Lisa would be early.

And she was.

"Your ten-fifteen is here, Mr. Calumet."

He actually ran a comb through his hair and wished he had some cologne to put on. "Please show her in."

Hugh rose when she appeared but remained a polite distance away, even though it was killing him to do so.

She looked much better than she had the last time he'd seen her. She'd gotten a job as a nurse in one of the big, regional hospitals in town and must've been going to her shift or coming back from it, because she was in a very cute set of pink scrubs, as well as sneakers with the same colors. Her eyes were clear, and her hair was glorious.

And she was still wearing his father's ring. He didn't know why that touched him so, but it did.

His fingers flexed with the need to bury them in it, but he diverted himself from those thoughts. "Would you like to sit down? Can I get you something? Water? Coffee? A drink?"

"It's a little early for a drink, Hugh, don't you think?"

He grinned a bit. "What happened to *Junior*?"

She took a seat in front of his desk, and he sat down in his big chair behind it.

"Well, that's kind of what I'm here about."

"Oh?" He couldn't begin to imagine what she was going to say, but he was going to enjoy the hell out of her presence while he had her.

"Yeah." Lisa wasn't at all sure how she was going to say this to him, but it was probably best—as in most things— just to come right out with it.

"I'm pregnant."

He looked dumbfounded, which she liked. A lot.

"It's mine?" he asked stupidly.

Lisa took immediate offense to that. It sounded just like the Hugh she knew and hated. "Did you see any other guys wandering around the mansion besides your father? Are you going to try to say that it's not? Because I'll get a paternity test—"

He could see things spiraling out of control. "No. I am not saying that at all. I'm just surprised. Pleasantly, but surprised."

"Pleasantly. Really." She sounded skeptical and was giving him side eye.

Hugh pushed himself away from his desk. "Yes." Then he asked, "But how do you feel about it?"

"I-I've always wanted children, but I never figured I'd be able to afford them. Thanks to your father, though, I can, if I want."

"And do you want?" he asked with incredible trepidation.

Lisa nodded, not looking at him but down at where her hands were on her barely-there belly. "Yes, I do. And I'm not here because I want anything from you. I don't."

"I know," he answered softly.

"But I can't imagine deciding to have a man's baby and not telling him." She gave him an impish look that reminded him—painfully—of how she used to be with his father. "Even you."

"Have you seen a doctor? Are you okay? Is the baby okay?"

"I'm just coming from my first checkup, which is later than it should be, but we used birth control and I shouldn't be pregnant. So, I ignored all of the signs, idiot that I am. Everything seems to be fine."

Hugh smiled, genuinely, for the first time in what seemed like a very long time. "That's wonderful. You got a new job as a nurse?"

"Yes, in my field and everything. It's a dream job, although I've been considering that I might want to move somewhere else, maybe somewhere warmer, where the baby can play outside year 'round without getting frostbite."

His face fell at that, and he fiddled with the papers on his desk nervously, which was something he rarely did because he rarely was.

"Would you keep your mind open to a counter proposal?"

Her eyebrow went up, and she actually smiled. "I don't know. Do you think I'll want to hear it?"

He flushed, looking abashed. "Well, probably not, since it comes from me."

She laughed at that, and he wallowed in the sound.

Hugh waited until her eyes met his naturally. "Marry me."

He counted it as a good thing that she hadn't burst out laughing as she might have, not long ago.

"I'm serious, Lisa. Marry me. It's the right thing to do." He cleared his throat and plowed on. "For what it's worth, and I know that's not much, I'm very sorry for how badly I treated you." He came around to the front of the desk, remaining a respectful distance away from her when all he wanted to do was to pick her up and carry her to the couch at the back of his office and make love to her—because that would be what it was for him, anyway, for the first time.

She was stumped more because she was stunned than anything else. Of course, she couldn't marry him—that would be ridiculous—but she hadn't expected him to say anything like that.

"And you know how much Father would have loved having a grandchild."

"He'll have one whether we marry or not, Hugh."

"Yes, but you could move back in. Even if we didn't marry, you could move back in. I have such wonderful memories of growing up in that house. I would love for my child to have those same memories. And a mother and a father, together."

She did love that house, too. Her new apartment was nice, but she had gotten spoiled. It was a bit cramped and would be even more so with all of a baby's stuff in it.

He couldn't believe that she seemed to be considering some of it. He'd take whatever he could get.

"And, if you're going to move in, well, we might as well get married."

Lisa snorted at that. "I don't follow your logic."

"We'll both be under the same roof, with our child. We both have the same tastes in the bedroom."

"Oh no! You are not spanking me again." Lisa actually got up, and he thought he was going to lose her and his child.

He was leaning back against his desk, and he didn't move one bit.

But he did say, "I seem to remember that that was something you enjoyed quite a lot, whether or not you wanted to admit it."

"I don't," she returned testily, still looking as if she was going to bolt any minute.

"Lisa," he intoned deeply.

"Hugh." She tried to sound unaffected, but she wasn't.

"Come to me."

She tsked, as if he was asking the world of her, but then, to his amazement, she slowly began to make her way to stand in front of him as he stood in front of her, slowly gathering her into his arms.

"I can't believe you're going to have my baby," he whispered reverently against her temple.

Lisa was still a bit stiff in his arms. "I can't believe I'm considering letting you talk me into moving in with you."

"Marrying me," he corrected firmly.

"Moving in with you."

Turns out scrubs are no protection against hardwood hands.

"Marrying you," she finally agreed, turning her face up for his kiss.

"I love you, Lisa."

She certainly hadn't expected to hear those words come out of his lips when he withdrew from the kiss.

"Don't say that, Hugh."

"Why not?" he frowned.

"Because you don't mean them." She was already teary eyed, and now she was actually crying.

He tipped her chin up, his lips hovering over hers. "Oh, but I do."

THE END

CAROLYN FAULKNER

The words "spanking" and "discipline" have always sent a shiver up Carolyn Faulkner's spine. She knows she's not alone. Writing started as a way to explore her feelings. Soon short stories flowed from her pen featuring reluctant heroes taking the leading lady in hand, but always for her own good.

Today Carolyn is the author of dozens of books. She writes from her home in Maine, where she lives with her husband and leading man.

You can read an interview with Carolyn here:
http://www.blushingbooks.com/blog/?p=175

You may check out her website while it's under construction here:
http://www.carolynfaulkner.com

Don't miss these exciting titles by Carolyn Faulkner and Blushing Books!

Series books
Military Daddies
Lieutenant Daddy
Captain Daddy
Colonel Daddy
Major Daddy

Gentle Series
Her Gentle Giant
Her Gentle Cowboy
Her Gentle Soldier
Her Gentle Gangster
My Book
The Alpha's Woman series
The Alpha's Woman
Kosh's Omega
Red's Mate
An Omega's Awakening
The Omega Within
Mate of the Omega Collection

Adored series
Adored
Tessa's Wedding

The Red Petticoat Saloon series
Grading Garnet

Thornton Brothers trilogy
AJ's Hope
Beau's Desire
Cade's Wish
Thornton Brothers, Three-Book Set

Taken as His series
Prima
Tria

Priceless Love series
Priceless

Love's Possession
Dangerous Love

Mistress Mommy Series
Alicia, Book One

Little Miss Series
His Little Miss
Little Francesca

Military Daddies
Captain Daddy
Lieutenant Daddy

Single Titles
Come to Me
The Gentleman Cowboy
Love Vs. Goliath
The Viking's Conquest
Second Chance Nanny
The Inconvenient Marriage
Promises, Promises
Love Cares Not
More Than All Right
Rescue Me
His Queen
Her King
Maddie and Daddy
Transgressions
The Brothers Rule
The Eye of the Beholder
Made to Order Bride
His Sugarbaby

Mr. Sunshine

No, Sir

His Runaway Bride

Undercover Sir

The Lark and The Bull

Doctor's Orders

A Babygirl for Christmas

Her Handyman

The Hart of the Matter

At His Hand

King of Hearts

True Desires

Lord Belden's Baggage

In His Care

Correct Me If I'm Wrong

Beauty Of The Beast

Tamed To His Hand

Daddy!

Amanda and the Stable Master

Lion

The Banished King

Northern Belle

The Cherished One

Forever Wife

Grace's Demon

Beauty's Beast

Captured by the Count

Male Order Bride

Sinful

Packed: The Enforcer

Submissive Love

A Heart Full of Heaven

Daddy's Girl

To Love a Man

Etta's Surrender

Her Secret Submission

Make Me

Let Me In

'Til Death Do Us Part

Promises Kept

The Obedient Wife

Old enough to Know Better

To Trust Her Heart

Naughty Girls: Brynn and Kim

After Hours: A Medical BDSM fantasy

Droit de Seigneur

Dutch and the Cowboy

Under the Lash

The Rogue and the Rose

Submissive Bride

The Unrequited Dom

Three's Company

All Hallow's Eve

The Reluctant Bride

His

Embraced

Attentions Throbbing

Submissive Desires

Kept

A Hard Man is Good to Find

The Spoils of War

Gilded Cage

Second Chances

Patriot Bride

The Boss of Her

Forever and Always

Tribute
Caged
The Substitute Wife
Captured by Time (w/ Alta Hensley)
A New Forever (w/ Alta Hensley)
Bound by Love: A Carolyn Faulkner Trilogy
Tears of a Vampire, and Vlad's Story, Two-Book Set
Never Say Never
Under the Cover of Love
Her Guardian Don
Her Knight In Faded Denim
Forever In Love
Depths of Desire
The Power Of Love
Only Her
On the Razor's Edge of Paradise
Indiscreet
A Most Unsuitable Mate
Make Me Yours
Ready For Love
The Gentleman Dom
The Supplicant
Belonging
Hidden Desires
Her Bad Boy
All Is Right With the World
The Error Of Her Ways
<u>At His Hand</u>

Holiday Stories
A Holiday to Remember
Griff's Christmas Angel
<u>A Season to Submit</u>

Anthologies
Tamed By The Cowboy
Blushing Cheeks Vol. 1
12 Naughty Days of Christmas2017
12 Naughty Days of Christmas 2021
Dominating His Valentine

BLUSHING BOOKS

Blushing Books is one of the oldest eBook publishers on the web. We've been running websites that publish spanking and BDSM related romance and erotica since 1999, and we have been selling eBooks since 2003. We hope you'll check out our hundreds of offerings at http://www.blushingbook s.com.

BLUSHING BOOKS NEWSLETTER

Please join the Blushing Books newsletter
to receive updates & special promotional offers.
You can also join by using your mobile phone:
Just text BLUSHING to 22828.